David Midgett

Mark Raney

ISBN: 978-0-578-02856-9

TO: W. T. CASPER

There have been Midgetts on these Islands from the beginning of time. Where they came from no one can say and the name very likely evolved from an ancient jest. It is not unreasonable to conjecture that a long time ago a formidable figure of a man washed ashore shipwrecked, naked even of a name. He stayed, and thereafter the Islanders wryly spoke of him as 'that midget' and so they called him Midgett. Then later some of the tribe wandered off these Islands. But rugged waterman they always are, and proud...

Paraphrased from The Hatterasman
by Ben Dixon Mac Neill

CHAPTER ONE

"Well?" Impatient. David Midgett sharply asking himself out loud, was he, would he, did he dare?

Then in several minutes. "Well." Resigned. Softly knowing that, yes he was, he would, he did dare. Knowing also that in the end desperation does finally reduce itself to no other alternative, to a single last resort. And knowing that this last alternative resort is always a damn dismal bitch of one, shrouded there darkly and smelling of dread and misery, and avoided hatefully until finally it absolutely no longer can be avoided however much dreaded and whatever the misery might bring. The dismal damn unavoidable bitch.

Then in several more minutes. "Well!" Chiding. Suddenly demanding harshly of himself, when, well when, was he going to make the first movement, that very first movement from which the thousand of other movements both big and little would stem and then flow steadily usually and surge sometimes, as with a tide that for small moments ceases and does neither outgoing or incoming and pauses as though deep in thought, contemplation even, until then finally deciding as though it also had an alternative, and having decided then begins to go the hell ahead and do either out or in with conviction, just as he had been pausing now thoughtfully while deciding, or making the pretense of it anyway and going

4

through the motions of it tide like what with no other alternative not actually. And his having decided after so long pausing, beyond contemplation and into meditation even, must now absolutely yes absolutely begin this the only course that this sea run will have until finally it concludes and reaches whatever happens happens, there at which ever end there will be to it. Because all of the tides of every kind mortal or other wise must run their full courses and always do, until whenever this sea run ends and wherever and why ever, and however this sea run ends at its end.

And here in this night of no moon and but few stars, the himself who was looking at himself in the dim blue wheelhouse light saw himself there before the big wheel stainless steel shining dim blue as blonde haired blown looking with a full beard that was rusted to a dirtish yellow grey now even at only thirty four, because of the lifetime of seawork certainly, and spread legged braced and flat footed planted, routinely, casually even, as a man standing the only proper stance for his workplace. As himself saw himself there in the dim blue reflection from the thick shatterproof glass that wrapped wide and all around except aft where there were separate wide windows in the fiberglass, as himself did pronounce out loud distinctly the three different "Wells" clearly and three times differently, and heard himself clearly the three times also, and saw himself pronounce them each distinctly in the forward glass with a no longer young innocent mouth that had now long since gone hard and was no longer boyish gently, long weathered by the brutal weather of blistering days and freezing nights and always and ever the constant wind the constant wind.

With the desperation of no other alternative now also adding a shadow of meanness, cruelty even, to his already too weathered mouth's hardness as his brutalized from a lifetime of seawork right hand appears suddenly as a low reflection in the forward glass, it dim blue also, rising now finally to seize the shining steel wheel with conviction while close behind his also brutalized left hand rises forward also but just below the actual seeing of it as a reflection forward. This after the third and last "Well! had chided sufficiently harshly and had reverberated sharply afterwards then only to fall down tumbling as a spentshot word upon the wheelhouse deck, after having done so very well its intended jarring duty, as his left hand finds the first of the two side by side keys ready and waiting there for the littlest of turns by scarred strong fingers.

Now one key then quickly the other key, that abruptly, rudely even, causes this big trawler to tremble herself while a brief though thorough shiver runs the length and breadth and the depth of her then passes and leaves behind only the tremble, as a separate heavy rumble begins low there deep inside at her bowels and rises heavily upwards, sluggishly even, until at last at long last, it seems, her twin monster diesels catch fully alive now with earnest thundering damn power yes power that is loud even at the beginning of it as it rises coming fast faster now like primed pump water, coming faster through pipes until it reaches the two mufflers that are as thick as small barrels there set on end and trusted skyward stack-like on either side and aft of the wheelhouse, that

6

itself is tiered more forward like a streamlined promontory and second story above the galley and the quarters that are spacious and below, until at the muffler's very topmost just above the wheelhouse the two jutting skinny by comparison tailpipes from the mufflers curve aft themselves and outboard a bit then flare gaped mouth and these begin to spew the sweet sickening diesel exhaust that now with earnest power below comes gushing. The first full belch of it is far blacker than even this night of no moon and but few stars, but a confined gusher it can only become since the exhaust can only hang milling and compacted about in this night cloud-like restricted and defined rather than streamer-like spreading and scattering and trailing and thinning, because there is not any trawler forward motion yet and because there is only a mere whisper of a moist sea wind. And this whisper wind silently in its enfolding arms holds the thundering engines noise and the trying to spew exhaust close about herself, this trembling still after the thorough shiver trawler, like a smothering invisible cloak of a something that is fierce and stifling.

While herself stands firm here to the channel side wood dock, lashed to it with a girl's wrist sized bowline and a likewise sized sternline that are pulled even more taunt and strummed string like now by the surging with full conviction for awhile and just flowing steadily later fresh incoming tide, that has begun to run its no alternative course, after having paused and decided as though that ever really mattered, and is going the hell ahead now and is doing its doing unseenly in this night and is everywhere rising creepingly and findingly and floodingly. Coming rushing so boldly now from the over yonder sea inlet that is two miles away as the wandering channel wanders forgetfully playfully, wistfully even, with all the many choices that it has before it doglegs itself into its straight purposeful down to business no nonsense stretch that ends at the inlet, that is actually only half mile away just over there beyond the mudflats and sloughs and the saltmarshes that become the sand bars and deep cuts and the mounding humping sand dunes as the grey soft seabirds fly it streaking and solitary and chest high to a man at dusk like a frantic winged thing that is being pursued. And increasingly possessive and domineering the tide is in its bold coming rushing, that is until it reaches this big trawler's hulking hull where it is sliced by herselfs' rugged cutwater without so much as a may I or a I beg your pardon, and is peeled off into tiny bubbles and a thin skim of foam there at the capped edges of the bulky body below of the coming the hell ahead tide, that is crowded and crammed in upon itself here whether it wants to be or not in rolling rolls as it is cutwater split and both sides are then forced herdlike to skirt this the wide slick trawler belly of herself, that is thrusted down the opposite of the muffler's up, and is thrusted deeply into itself the tide like some kind of massive unyielding plow until finally it passes herself the intruder where here this bold tide is allowed by herself to come once again back together but only if slappingly so done like two swift identical halves that are allowed to resound in their rejoinment and doing so quite happily with a passing thank you ma'am of whirls and swirls as

8

though nothing had happened.

And if it had all is forgiven now anyway, here at the blunt white cliff like rising from dark water broad assed stern of herself, her trembling self, where stands slack Oscar here in this night of no moon and but few stars there upon the sturdy wood dock all dangley armed and warped legged and smashed faced, with the smashed face resulting from when the saltwood weighing a ton trawl door had jerked free of its deck holding bracket and had swung violently because of a violent sea roll and got him smack but goddamn good and bloody, like smacking a ripe pumpkin broadside with a table top smack. And leaving Oscar thereafter utterless and stupid, though seawise still yes that certainly and still and probably more so now than before the faithful smack, standing there old and stomped on ugly and loyal always and worthless away from trawlers at sea, while being worth any two of the best sea men when upon her deck and being priceless there. But tugging now and puffing from the tugging long and hard on the tide taunt strummed string sternline, until slowly and finally bringing herself dockside closer by mere inches, but enough just enough so he could snatch free the girl's wrist size sternline up and up and over the creosoted dock piling while in the same motion tossing it into an overturned basket looking pile upon the broad sterndeck. Then jolting himself into a semblance of uprightness and beginning to warp leg his smashed faced and dangley armed old loyal seawise self forward by comical spasms, toward herself's bow where just beyond her bowline circled strum taunt the piling that is there, and is where Oscar halts and stands then looks up utterlessly and loyally at the chest and the. shoulders and the bearded face and the blond hair of our too weathered sea captain. There bust-like perched in the wheelhouse's dim blue light and rigid looking, immortal looking even as if of granite, and spread legged braced and flat footed-planted. There pronouncing his three so different "Wells" outloud to the himself that he sees in the thick glass windshield's reflection, and seeing himself and hearing himself doing them here before the stainless steel big wheel, while cast so rigid and dim blue with his brutalized right hand still gripped to the wheel while his brutalized left hand has long since left the second ignition key.

Those first real movements of the hundreds and the thousands of movements that will follow each other in sequence as though predestined until whenever and wherever and whyever and however this searun ends at its end. And now the left hand rests lightly encompassly upon the close side by side throttle levers, until abruptly and without plan or so much as a conscious thought he pulls them both back gently simultaneously, and with this gently throttling down pull, as if by remote control magic the heavy rumble below and aft and at the mufflers eases considerably and softens significantly although herself the trawler continues to tremble if only slightly now. As slack Oscar assumes he is being given the signal that the idling engines means that here are those brief moments just prior to our sea captain's going into gear and revving a bit, and then pulling ahead and away from the dock this searun toward its unforeseeable end having begun. That isn't the signal that signal at least, not this time though it should have been and had always been before, but this time is merely a knee jerk instinct reaction thing of our sea captain done while himself ponders so lost in thought beyond contemplation and into meditation even. But Oscar can't know this, how could he and who would expect him to, and so he slips the bowline up and up and over the piling at the beginning of the idle, the false signal, and tosses its bulk with the same motion to pile in the bow upturned basket like as the sternline had been piled for later stowing away. Then instead of scrambling aboard before being left behind Oscar simply stands there loyally looking his stomped priceless usual self on the wood dock in this night of no moon with a sorely hurt pride at not going along also showing as bright disappointment and incomprehension in his normally dull eyes that always now remained vacant and without the light of strong emotion, except for this time.

As our dim blue sea captain up there bust-like in the perched wheelhouse startles with an easily seeable startle jump, a frantic approaching panic jump even, and loudly pronounces yet a fourth different "Well!!" that is a shout of pending nearing bad serious danger that demands, commands even, a flurry series of quick sure corrections before it is too late and the damage is done like spilt milk or closing the barn door afterwards and so incorrectable. And this "Well!!" reverberates also, as the others had reverberated, however this one through sheer force and urgency refuses to fall down upon the wheelhouse deck after doings its intended as it rolls thunderlike back and forth back and forth within this small dim blue closed space though diminishing ever so gradually slightly with each back and forth roll as our no longer cast rigid but still bust-like perched sea captain becomes all frantic panic action now with his big sure proper movements. Because with herself the trawler freed too soon and unexpectedly from her remaining tether lashing by our assuming Oscar and idling uselessly out of gear, the coming in a hell of a rush tide suddenly snatches herself toy-like from the wood dock, with the bow suddenly arc swinging crazily around like a play boat in a small boy's swirling tub, and heads herself directly quickly, as though propelled, toward the shoals and the stumps and the debris at the near far bank. Until our sea captain finally suddenly awakens and returns from meditation and is now animated and full spins to starboard the big wheel and slams hard both gear levers hard forward and then urgently nudges both throttle levers slightly forward, then a bit more forward, then a bit more still, until the below and the aft rumble tremble rises and rises and thickens and widens and becomes a single fiercely rising louder engine noise, that now screams of power and push and mightiness all around inside the dim blue wheelhouse, and outside also spreading rock tossed into pond wave-like out and out into this night of but few stars. As slowly, ever so slowly, breath holding suspenseful slowly, herself her thunder rumbling self slows and slows then ceased entirely her all wrong swinging arc and direction, only to hesitate now for seemingly endless moments as though suspended there on the final inches of a cliff above danger. Then, and again slowly, she begins her battle charge and clanging engagement, her hand to hand combat, to finally stall then overpower then subdue itself, this fast coming tide. As himself, our all sure movemented sea captain, proceeds through a pure blur of motions as he slams both gear levers from forward to reverse, while ignoring the possibility of stripping them as just a calculated risk, and pour on both throttle levers full bore in a frantic wild backing away suddenly of churning violently foamy water, and spins the stainless steel wheel maddeningly hard aport. Then and just as quickly as he has done all that he undoes it, by the coming off from full throttle momentarily then the opposite spinning of the big wheel and the going back to hard forward from hard reverse, to win finally decisively this battle and to withdraw triumphantly from the dangerous edge. As the violently churning section of the tide passes as boiling foam on down channel, to be lost in this night of no moon, and is replaced by a tamed controlled rushing water that is now propelled by a mechanical power far mightier than the tide's own, since it is so concentrated and so aimed, though tiny even by comparison and less mighty and certain and endless in the larger perspective. As the now righted and properly-directed trawler returns to the channel middle and the safety that is there in front of the wood dock, where still stands slack Oscar, but now also looking surprised and concerned and puzzled by what had just occurred so dramatically so suddenly, in addition to his already incomprehension look and his sorely hurt pride showing brightly as disappointment at not going along.

As herself the trawler now begins to show off shamelessly by becoming absolutely majestic and beautiful, the hussy, as her proud bow raises itself in a white water splitting and rolling away of the coming tide, and her stern settles itself lower for its prolonged and steady and serious business, with himself still dim blue before the wheel, bust-like immortal and perched there as he is, and much weathered with his blonde hair blown and his full beard more grey now, while spread legged braced and flat footed planted as though cast that way at his workplace, with both brutalized hands now gripped to the shining wheel before the thick glass forward. As bewildered Oscar continues to look on there, jilted and left behind, upon the wood dock under this night as herself with himself atop, and majestic also, begins to pass in review before this audience of but one.

Underway at long last and ghostly there white passing and large upon the black rushing water, like some trembling rumbling mirage, with her tall tapered iron pipe outriggers stretched high up and a little out boastfully, braggartly even, and cable winched vee-like and locked gear secured in that configuration to silently shout proclaim "Victory!" to each and to all. And these bold arms are painted red for a long way up, then are blue tipped, and are thrusted black night skyward, thin and stark, as they rise from a common base of pale white. These same arms that when winch lowered and locked horizontally abeam opposing, and therefore ready for their real intended business, become separate and deadly arms each with its own trawl for her prowling self, this long haul trawling beast, who snatches and snares and dredges in these two death nets all and every living thing within their wide trawling swatch. Arms that are never raised vee-like when upon the sea because of the top heaviness of them, but are always raised once inside the inlet because top heavy no longer matters what with the gentler swells there and because who the hell wants to swipe off everything, outriggers included, within their long arms' reach and path whether other boats or docks or channel markers or thick foliage upon a near bank. This same common base from which also begins, literally, a shrouding maze aloft of steel cables and lines and ropes that each are highly specialized and very functional and are of so critical an importance in their duties and responsibilities, and now that herself with himself are underway at long last these, all these, begin a low whisper rustling of noise, a murmuring among themselves, then a steel against steel and steel against iron low clatter among themselves, with rope against anything adding a thudding bumping bass chorus,and begins then also a strange singing of sorts, a low and growling and haunted even singing, as the forward motion wind begins to pass faster and faster and stronger among them all, rippling them, vibrating them, strumming them, even as the docking tethers had been strummed tautly, this as herselfs' increased speed increases.

And all of these night sights and sounds and moods and feelings are in this pale scene as it continues to pass gliding, floating nearly, in review ghostly white now and even approaching an abhorrence spell as in a veiled midnight's restless dream of red and blue atop white and thrusted skyward on a background of sheer black, for all and left behind on the dock Oscar to see. Poor Oscar, our slack Oscar, with his smacked ugly face unaccustomed to reflecting so many unfamiliar emotions so quickly, like a hardened plastic mask that is heatedly forced into moldability against its will against its nature by the great weight and the great impact of circumstances. Oh yes, but above and beyond and down deep inside, still seawisely knowing what all bluewatermen know and have known and will always know, knowing that more important than all else and everything, a sea captain, any sea captain, does not ever go far out upon her blue alone, all alone, in a boat of whatever length and breadth and state of modernness, for any reason or excuse or circumstance however great, that is if that sea captain values and cherishes his boat and her gear and his life, that is unless that sea captain is hopeless about or disgusted with either or all three foolishly, and is no longer in the least caring about real dangers and their consequences. But what could Oscar do after having been so rudely jilted and left behind to puzzle and to worry and to nurse hurt pride, after have been told "No, not this trip!" flatly simply sharply at the usual food and fuel loading, that was then followed by a really thoughtless hateful "Stay here!" from our back turned and preoccupied and walking away sea captain, speaking this second cruel slap this unnecessary slap, which did not explain or justify or defend anything either, just as the first cruel slap had not done any of this never ever going far out upon her blue alone, and was the end of this one sided conversation.

And Oscar could only stand jilted back stunned, there upon the wood dock, and wobbly and silently do as he had been told to do because he always had and he always would because our sea captain was his true friend, his only friend, his employer, his landlord, his guardian. But foremost he was his captain, the final authority, and Oscar could and would, matter of factly without so much as a second thought, give his life at the moment of a blue sea crisis if by so doing so easy and so generous an act this could mean that his captain might live or that herself the trawler might live, should either or both become placed in mortal jeopardy. But first verbally slapped and jilted and then left behind it could never and would never come to that, not on this trip that was for whatever secretive purpose to wherever mysterious destination with the underway proceeding accordingly now without solitary there Oscar.

As herself, her ghostly majestic self, comes abeam of the first outbound channel marker light beyond the wood dock, that begins a zigzag line of green then red then green again, first starboard then port, then starboard again, lights that are spaced widely apart in a planned sequence series that forms a corridor between them to guide safely inland of her far deep, at least, any and all who dare venture to or from her at night, himself and herself included. This pale procession of but a single entrant, with himself still a bluish bust though becoming smaller, there atop white on a background of black and dimming and fading and blurring now with the distance. Until just at the final point of no longer being visible at all by Oscar, our sea captain spins the big stainless steel wheel a hard wheeling short starboard spin that abruptly turns herself from the long and the wandering channel into a longer and a straighter, straight as a shot even, channel-that goes directly to the inlet. And along this straighter channel, sandbars and seagrass islands and wide cuts and sand dunes gradually and grandly rise and replace the mudflats and the saltmarshes and the sloughs, as a red then a green marker light leads zigzag alternatingly one to the other and yet another outward bound, in the opposite of red right returning the bluewaterman's axiom, until himself and herself come almost abeam of the last channel marker, the goodbye marker, the fair wind and a fast ship marker, the good voyage marker, where beyond the bar is, where the final line is. And it is here that our sea captain quickly throttles back to dead idle and adrift and disappears from view even as only a bust and reappears astern full figured and tall upon the work deck amid the conglomeration of gear, and in only a flurry of several moments' sure activity of winching and locking he has both outriggers down horizontal and secure abeam opposing, and then quickly again appears again bust sized and bluish there in his perch and throttles up and corrects for the drift and returns once again to the proper channel course for crossing the bar, the final line, where beyond only the belled buoy is rolling and tolling the wide deep sea.

And here we are, all of these sights and sounds and moods and feelings here in this night of no moon and but few stars, with the four distinct and so very different "Wells" having been spoken and now are over and done and gone, all spent, so what else is there for himself to say now even to himself, now outward bound for sure and committed and underway toward the whenever and the wherever and the whyever and the however end of this bold searun that has begun now for sure, for sure, in all of its far seriousness and consequence.

CHAPTER TWO

Herself struck bottom when midway across the bar, a sliding glancing bump thump only, though that was more a friendly reminder nudge to toll the presence of the waiting below menace destroyer, rather than a hard threatening damage blow, and it served to again remind himself of the narrowness and the shallowness and the shiftiness and the treachery that is the Bogue Inlet bar, that is never always the same shape or at the same depth with its peaks and its valleys that rise and fall so swiftly so unpredictably that a depth recorder there is useless with its only limited forward range and because of this quick running blindly among hazards. The peaks are called sinkers because by the time you know that they are there you are sunk, and this treachery is constant whether fair weather or foul weather and is there through all of the tides continually whether high tide or low tide and whatever phase the moon is in and each tide in itself varies dramatically in its degree and in its intensity. Just a friendly thump reminder to be certain that David Midgett remembered and understood that which had been drummed instilled into him since first trawling as a boy with his dad, that all trawler floundering except those few that are sudden violent squall caused offshore always happen here at the sea captain's door step at his very own inlet's bar and whether inbound or outbound and more especially so and more particularly so and so frequently recorded as so down through all the generations for the past five hundred years here along the ragged jagged North Carolina coastline that has long long been infamous and dreaded to bluewatermen. And with the sinkers' bump reminder David said out loud "I know you're there" simply that as he always did and with this himself and herself were then safely across the bar and into bluer water and coming up on the sea buoy, where with the bobbing buoy off herself's port bow David came right slowly with the big wheel, and this course change caused the compass that floats in its alcohol world to swing and to dip wateryly briefly in its sealed housing, and then he eased both throttle levers forward a bit until herself's sea cruising and best planning speed was reached.

And with this the horribly eroded inlet point of land that is at Emerald Isle came directly astern and the five mile squat sand mass that is Bear Island came off starboard, and then both of these gradually began to lower and to dim into the distance into the black all around background here in this night. And now away from the land and steadily leaving it farther and farther off starboard and astern, the evening haze that clung just above the land and all along it to just offshore every evening every spring began to thin and then to recede also until it too was left behind as everything else and Oscar also had been left behind. And now beyond this haze, the few stars that had been, multiplied quickly and became many stars, and if they still were not at their brightest at least not yet they did have a sharper glow and a better precision about themselves and they would brighten and sharpen even more later on until finally becoming quite precise and very many. And it would be just after midnight when the crescent sliver of the moon that would appear did appear. And here offshore the sea breeze that rose every evening every spring at around nine o'clock to blow away the overland haze and to cool the land there did rise once again in this night and it came up suddenly from only a point or two off herself's proud bow, and with this arisen sea breeze the sea swells that while were not dead calm by any means still were far from the bad rolling and the hard pitching swells that would demand himself's undivided attention to herself's course and stability. Herself whom himself had named Bright Dawn because he thought that certainly she would be, at herself's launch christening only two years before, though a lifetime ago it now seemed what with all the terribleness that has taken place, and more so recently, like a terrible train gathering momentum on a long downhill run.

This since that gay fun happy day when the federal man's banker had taken title to Evening Star himself's old and lumbering and much loved wood trawler as a trade in, but only so it could be sold for salvage because it was pitifully outdated and sadly inefficient, in return for the then completed Bright Dawn that was the most modern long haul trawler available worldwide and truly the state of the art to the last functional detail. But, and this but was an enormous but, also came with the really staggering mortgage, at least to those not accustomed to dealing in those terms, of one million dollars, though this price would be inexpensive at twice that price when the cash crop harvesting potential is considered. And besides the ideal of no mortgage or even an inexpensive mortgage in this day and time is just that, an ideal, and reality is hardly ever as we wish and is never perfect or risk free, as in a marriage where there is for better or for worse in sickness and in health, also, with trust and hope as vital an ingredient in the marriage ceremony as they are vital in the mortgage ceremony, and both ceremonies are little more than huge gambles on the future that each venture on its own will turn out to be practical and manageable and wise.

So this simple trade, Evening Star for Bright Dawn plus mortgage, did take place finally and at long last even, after the months and months of high pressure convincing and hearty salesmanship tactics by the federal man that such a trade was absolutely and positively in David's best interest and in the commercial fishing industry's best interest and in even North Carolina's best interest as well as in the best interest of the whole damn United States of America by God and while we are at it in the best interest of the ever loving bloody goddamn entire world and its conglomeration of underdeveloped nations and its developing nations and its developed nations, whew, and each time the federal man climbed upon the soap box and gave his pitch he became carried away by the flow of his own words and he became heady and dreamlike and breathless. This conglomeration of nations with their sprawling crawling doubling tripling quadrupling swarming mankind populations that doggedly insist upon fucking endlessly and without controls of any kind, except rarely, and with wild abandon ramming and cramming and church condoned without a single thought or care that the multitudes of the new young mouths that result floodingly yearly must be fed daily and daily again and again and daily again for each and every day of their multitudeous lifetimes however long or short that these lifetimes may be what with mass starvation now so real and so common a plague.

So how could David refuse as insistent and as lofty an argument as this one and who would expect him to refuse staggering mortgage and all, good with the bad with the failability of foresight being what it is in comparison to hindsight, without having heavily upon his conscious the weighty responsibility for all present and future generations of swarming mankind and their millions and billions with the total numbers spinning higher and higher crazily like a run away calculator gone tilt, and trillions even of shrunken bodies with glaring eyes and swollen bellies that would again and again night after night go belly grumbling fiercely to restless sleep empty, if David refused the trade and by so doing became a hardened and callous traitor not only to himself but also to his industry and to his State and to his Nation and to the entire bloody World by God.

So David did not refuse, how could he, and then the background applause became thunderous and the federal man smiled happily and his banker smiled happily and they both shook David's hand gladly and they pounded his back warmly and they loudly proclaimed that our David was indeed being true to himself and was a comrade to his industry and a patriot to his State and to his Nation and a proper farmer of the sea to the World, and Jesus what a beautiful and a heartwarming scene that trade was, and it only two years ago. Herself whom here tonight himself brings right again slowly with the big wheel again, but by only a honing bit this time, with himself becoming accurate now with himself becoming the serious navigator now. And coming right to a watery swinging dipping compass heading of south southwest two hundred and thirty degrees outbound which would make the inbound heading fifty degrees, the difference being the straight line of one hundred and eighty degrees while also allowing for wind and for drift each way. With this searun taking place far inside the interior of the huge curve that is the vast concave that is named Onslow Bay, that is not a bay in the protected enclosure safe harbor sense, but is a bay in the larger than a cove yet smaller than a gulf geographical sense, and is the indented underside below Raleigh Bay that is not, yet is, a bay for the same reasons and is where the barren sand strips that are the windy Outer Banks begins to recede from their outermost deep sea incursion at Cape Hatteras.   With this underside of Onslow Bay itself going from the headland at Cape Lookout to the headland at Cape Fear, and including one third of North Carolina's rugged coastline and one hell of a lot of unruly open ocean.

   With himself heading herself steadily now into the yawning openness of it and steadily toward the unseeable and the untouchable and the only chart plotable intersecting point that, is named thirty four degrees fifty minutes latitude and seventy seven degrees twenty five minutes longitude, by and for those who have a definite need to know and a sure reason for going there, that is thirty five nautical miles off shore and is midway between Bogue Inlet and New River Inlet and is literally in himself's front yard when it is considered that long haul trawlers frequently trawl offshore to ten times that distance. So that this searun will be like the man who goes strolling for the newspaper across his own front yard, with himself now having begun his own stroll towards thirty four and a half and seventy seven and a quarter, which is merely down by the watermeter and before the sidewalk and to the right of the shrubbery and just beyond the big oak tree and at a place point known well to himself.

"Don't start with me about Oscar," he said to himself . Then he said, "I just don't want to hear it about Oscar," as though that would end the conversation before it really had begun and before it began to irritate him by reminding him about that something that he did not want to think about or even to remember. That something being a very sore subject to himself and for now better left swept aside in his thinking as it had been and safely there out of the way.

'But it was wrong what you did to Oscar, and it was wrong the way that you did it to him, he thought, as the conversation with himself continued. 'Among the things that you are not as a man, you are not a cruel man,' he thought.

"He couldn't be a part of this and he shouldn't be a part of this, this is for me to do and for me to do alone and that's all there is and was to it. All right?" he said. But with the conversation with

26

himself really just beginning and soon to become relentless and long, before finally ending.

'But why the cruelty? The cruelty was not needed, nor was the cruelty necessary. It was like spanking a child without reason or need or necessity.'

"Oscar had to understand quickly and plainly that he couldn't come, and I didn't have all night to explain over and over to him where I was going and why I was going and why he couldn't come along."

'But you could have been gentle in the way you handled it with Oscar.'

"Among the things I 'm not as a man, is, I'm also not a gentle man. There just isn't a place in commercial fishing for a gentle man."

'But there is a place in commercial fishing for fair men, we can agree on that. And you have always been a fair man before.'

"All right, okay, I was wrong in the way I handled it with Oscar. But it's done now, and I can't change it. And I just don't want to hear this, not this and not now, not on top of everything else."

'Because everything about all of this is wrong, and deep inside you know that it is all wrong and it is that all wrongness that has made you irritable and preoccupied. It looks wrong, and it sounds wrong, and it feels wrong, and it smells wrong, and it tastes wrong. All wrong because it is exactly that , all wrong.'

"It's business, only that. Only business."

'But it is not your kind of business, and it is not you. And you do not have any business doing this kind of business,' he thought.

"Finally it just came down to my doing this because there wasn't any other choice," he said, getting harrowed a bit by the relentlessness of his own other self.

'No, you are wrong. There are always other choices. Always other avenues, other options.'

"Not this time, finally this was my only choice."

'You could have quit. You did your best, so you could have simply quit and walked away from it as having failed after having done your best. Let them take the boat, let them have it. You could have done that. However much you want to keep this particular boat, you can always get another boat later, one exactly like this one. Better man that you have admitted and accepted failure and quit and walked away, accepting the loss of whatever it was that they had risked and therefore had to lose that they did not want to lose, before they would allow themselves to get into wrong businesses such as this now is a wrong business.'

"Among the other things I'm not as a man, is I'm not a failure man or a quitter man or a walker away man. There isn't a place in commercial fishing for men such as those, just as there isn't a place in it for gentle men."

'Now you are being idealistic, and worse, you are being romantic. There is a place in commercial fishing for being practical and realistic, just as there is a place for these in every other endeavor. And walking away was definitely a choice, and your best choice, had you chosen realistically.'

"No, walking away was never a real choice. Walking away would be for a different type of man than I have been and am."

'But you can do this instead, with this calling for a different type of man than you have been and am?'

"I can keep this boat by doing this instead of that, so I'm, doing this instead of that, whatever different type of a man that this calls for."

'This different type of man is a far less likable type of a man, to yourself as well as to others, than that different type of a man would ever be.'

"None of this is my fault," he said, becoming defensive. "I just reacted to the situation that I was forced into, and to the alternative that was presented for me to get out of that situation. Blame the first group of "they," with the federal man at the head of the list and by far the worst of the lot. They are the ones who betrayed me, and with their betrayal makes this choice, the choice I've made, the right choice. So blame them. The second group of "theys" merely presented the alternative. And they are sending their wares to me to haul and they are handing them to me on a silver platter, and they aren't making me go too far or through too much to get them. It' short and it's sweet, I haul their wares, I keep this boat. And it's only business."

'You are wrong that a right naturally follows a wrong, that isn't the way it works, ' he thought, still in relentless pursuit but closing. 'Each is separate is not related, the one does not justify the other. The second group of "theys" are not doing this to help you, nor in anyway to make this easier for you. They do what they do for themselves only, and with absolutely no concern for others. And they will betray you far more quickly and far more ruthlessly than the first group of "theys" did. That first betrayal was merely political. The Democrats were out, the Republicans were in, only that. When the administrations changed, the policies changed also. The wind shifted, only that. Those men, those first "theys" never go against the wind, and you should have realized that from the start. That is what they are as men, and who they are as men, and how they are as men. And it is merely politics to them, the way of things to them, an expediency to them, their own survival means within their own chameleon system to them. But never do they consider their expediency as a betrayal, they just do not deal in such personal terms. And you should have realized that also. But these "theys," these second "theys," they are truly mean "theys" and very personal betrayal "theys." And they will not stop at anything or for anyone no matter what in order to gain their wrong end. They are sending their wares nearby to you and are handing their wares to you on a silver platter for their own very selfish business reasons. You are no more to them than a mule. And you will never be other than that to them. A mule that they have hired to haul their wares, because they never touch their wares themselves. They do not need to, because there are always greedy men such as yourself who will gladly do the touching of the wares for them in return for a price.'

"Well, yes there is much I failed to realize going in, that only now am I beginning to realize. And later will probably begin to realize even better. And there are many things assumed then without question, that now I would never assume even after lengthy questions. But this searun comes down to this bottom line, finally and simply, that while greed and ruthlessness aren't the rule in commercial fishing, neither are they uncommon to it. And I have practiced them both at various times and to various degrees in my fishing life as well as in my life apart from fishing however little there is and has been of that. And since I have been forced now to choose between two different types of men to become, with both in far extreme of what I have been and am, the only choice that I can make is on the side that represents those with which I at least have similarities. With that side I can at least relate to the familiarities that exist between us. So it is with the second "theys" that I must side. Because walking away because of chameleon politics and chameleon politicians, those first "theys" who can never be condoned or even tolerated, well, that walking away would be just too bitter of a thing to do, though a time may come when I am forced to do that also however bitter. So siding with them would now be just too foreign and unfamiliar, there not existing any similarities between us." he said, rallying his conviction to block the closing in and to defend successfully against the relentlessness of his own other pursing self. "You see, the second "theys" promised nothing, while offering the money that is an out, so betrayal by them if it happens would be only business. But the first "theys," well, they promised the rainbow that would be for the good of all mankind, and their betrayal, the betrayal that did actually happen, that betrayal is unpardonable."

'Then you really have decided, and your choice is made without doubts,' he thought, suddenly resigned now and fully, yet trying one last try however lamely. 'But the door has not yet slammed to make this choice irreversible,' he thought. 'You can still spin this big wheel, turning herself around, while you search for yet a third option. Consider well ,just as you did while we were still lashed to the wood dock. Consider well, and once again.'

"No. This searun has begun, " he said, and it had.

'But it still is not too late.'

"Yes. Now it is too late," he said, and it was.

Himself, who, having swung forward his captain's chair that is pedestalled and is silent jointed and is upon a long swivel arm and extends from a recess, is now seated and is relaxed though ever ready before the shining dim blue stainless steel wheel beyond which is the sweeping control panel layout that is like a space commander's console with its several levels of rows of labeled switches, each with their own on and off and malfunction light, and its banks of dials by engine group and its banks of meters by engine group and its banks of gauges by engine group, and even with its miniaturized and versatile computer. And beyond this layout as well as above this layout as well as to either side of this layout is the bracketed and the shockproof and the waterproof array of electronic boxes that make Bright Dawn so very advanced and truly the state of the art worldwide in trawlers. Because these boxes include herself's own several marine radios for short or long or for longer range, and herself's own Loran that utilizes satellites for navigation, and herself's own various specialized recorders and calibrators, and herself's own television system that monitors the engine room as well as the sterndeck work area from different angles. And especially because these boxes include herself's own sonars, those indispensable twenty first century innovative sonars, that enable the so distinct and the very profitable advantage over all competitors who are without their invaluable service. These sonars that are capable of sending back to the monitors, television pictures of the ocean floor as well as the trawl nets that are deployed and trawling as well as the flounder or the shrimp or the mullet or the sea trout, or whatever it is that has schooled and is traveling at whichever particular season at whichever particular location, that is the prey at that particular time and is to be electronically sought and seized, after but brief moments of homing in and getting the fix then preying upon the prey. Prey that at least used to stand a resemblance of a fair chance of escape, and therefore for survival, with the very worst that could happen being that a school was one time only thinned considerably as the prey scattered and dodged or compacted and dodged by natural instinct, which was pitted one on one against the sea captain' s experience and his hunting instincts, so that the odds of the chase and capture were balanced usually except whenever the balance was tipped one way or the other way to favor the really quick and keen or to favor simply the luckiest.

But prey that now with the likes of herself and cold boxes stands absolutely no chance of escape and therefore no chance for survival, except as strays in small clusters fleeing here and there, now that luck and quickness and keenness are no longer factors for the prey, because the electronic eyes see everything, and even the prey's instinct is no longer a factor because none of these are any longer essential for the sea captain, so therefore no longer effective for the prey. And an entire school of prey can simply disappear from the monitor's screen and reappear in a trawler's hold in but the brief length of a trawl and the retracing of that trawl and the retracing of that retracing while minor navigational corrections are made to correct for the school's frantic dodgings, that are depicted so clearly and so coldly upon the screen with the degree of success in thousands of pounds of harvest now depending solely upon the captain's electronic technician's skills that are textbook and classroom learned and no longer depending upon his sea captain's sea experience and sea instinct skills, that can only be learned through endless trial and error and by becoming one with the prey and by much time spent at preying at sea.

Himself, dim blue still in the wheelhouse light and reflecting bustlike as just that in the wrapped wide and all around forward glass and perched there inside the second story promontory with a wide vista of the panorama all around from either side to forward and to the far horizon as well as all around above. As herself's proud bow rises and falls slowly heavily repetitively amid the steadily coming rolling swells, and the bright star shine that reflects upon all this rolling sea surface is like flickering crystal flashes in a broad wavy mirror. As himself's brutalized left hand appears low and forward in the glass and then methodically begins to turn off labeled switches one by one click, click, click, click, methodically, until one by one the radios are off and the radar is off and the Loran is off and the sonars are off and until all exterior lights are off including the running lights and even the dim blue wheelhouse light is off until finally, methodically, the only on lights anywhere on board are the tiny white compass light and the stark engine room light that shows the frozen grey inanimate scene that is there upon the shaded monitor that is above and recessed and way over to the left. As herself with himself continues to proceed steadily toward thirty four and a half and seventy seven and a quarter, that place point pencil dot upon a chart place that is within the huge concave that is the vast Onslow Bay, with herself still looking ghostly there white passing and large upon the black all around background and approaching an abhorrence spell even as in a veiled midnight's restless dream, with himself no longer visible even as dim blue bustlike and herself visible only as a figment thing, as I thought I saw thing, as an almost thing.

.   'Nor were you ever gentle with Mary,' he thought, with a deeper understanding now of the two sides that are himself. 'Just as you were not gentle with Oscar back there upon the wood dock. Not ever gentle with Mary, not really. Tender, yes you were sometimes tender with Mary during the moments of love making and during the telling her of your affection. But gentle, no not ever gentle. Because it simply is not a part of you to behave mild in temperament toward anyone to any real extent. Because the first thing a fisherman learns is that the sea does not care. That she will calm and she will gale, that she will provide and she will withhold. But through none of these does she ever care. And after having lived sufficiently long with such a constant sea, the fisherman becomes constant also. And just as the sea has moments of tenderness and moments of rage, so does the fisherman. Because they have become as one. Because that is the absolute way of things with the sea and her men.

'Mary, who came like a fair breeze to you during an afternoon of warm rain in early summer. Mary, who brought with her the triumphant smile of a new young woman now home once again from college until fall. Who fresh laughed her teenager no longer and never again posed way so completely into your man's work and world life so unexpectedly as you were in the lounge down at Capt. Charlie's Restaurant on the waterfront and standing at the long cedar bar that was lined three deep seated and standing with charter boat captains and clammers and trawler captains and gillnetters and long line captains and crabbers, while all of you self-appointed heroes were half smashed from many beers and loudly bragging coarsely and together as usual about the dangerousness and the profitableness and the manliness of your separate and equally demanding sea and sound professions. Mary, who came happily reunited with the special group of her high school girlfriends as they seated themselves while chatting gaily around the large table that was away from the long cedar bar and across the room beside the bandless bandstand. Mary, whose hair was the shiny blonde that yours had been at her age, though her hair was naturally curly and yours had never been, and it was cut medium length and it fitted snugly about her face and neck in a gathering of loose and blowing soft curls. Mary, with the scattered splash of little freckles all over on her recently sun browned arms and face and shoulders, with good lips of pinkish and bright eyes of bluish, and wearing so preciously the yellow print cotton sun dress that was cut low but low just enough. Mary, young woman now and teenager never again, who you could not get through the crowded crowd to talk with quickly enough, tumbling and fumbling and mumbling as you came charging, who when you did and were boldly seated beside her, totally ignored you with such maddening ease and charm. But Mary, whose cold rebuffs you did witheringly endure that afternoon, who at the proper time after proper homage and after proper persistence did allow herself to be grudgingly won over by the romantic aura of the solitary sea captain that new young women find so immediately irresistible but will never admit. Who did come hand in hand with you at rainy dusk down to the dock to see your Evening Star, and who had the normal dry landers awkwardness in managing the stubby passageways and the cramped rooms. Mary, suited in Oscar's foul weather gear, and standing so young body close beside you with the two of you breathless and now so suddenly in love there upon the upswept rising bow of that earlier proud herself that faced the deep moving channel there in the wet and the warm wind in the coming night. Mary, our Mary, who in the first year of the marriage gave birth to the blondest ever of sons, and he was the big footed and the big handed and the fresh laughed and the little baby freckled perfect blend of you both. But the same Mary, who went forever from you while crying mad tears of hard sorrow during a grey afternoon of raw rain in the late winter of that next year.

'And when her outburst did come after the reasons for it were so long in the building and then so long in the festering, it came fully, and it came finally, as our Mary shouted, "Pity is all I feel for you!" Who then went on hatefully even, "Because you are a pitiful man, David!" Mary, who was dark and trembling with madness and with sorrow. "You are rude with everyone. And you can't be at ease anywhere. Because all you think about is being at sea in your boat. And when you are you are gone for days or weeks at a time without any concern for what these absences and their uncertainty do to me. When you are home, and then for only a day or two, you drink beer constantly as though you would rather be someone else somewhere else. And if you aren't down at the boat getting it ready, then you are down at Capt. Charlie's with your buddies. When we are rarely alone, you are preoccupied and irritable and extreme, David! And when we make love, there's a detachment, a brevity, to it as though having given so much emotion elsewhere, there isn't much left for me." Her eyes blinking rapidly from the strain of knowing where such talk was leading. "Such a man, you David!, deserves only contempt for his smallness, and pity for his narrowness. Your boat and your sea and what your trawl are not loving and sharing and feeling things. But I am, and your son is, and your mom is. But there's so little room in you for us, David. How dare you do this to us! And how dare you do this to yourself. Your mom didn't have a choice, she had to accept such selfishness from your dad. She says you have become exactly like him. And that this with you is like a rerun from thirty years ago. But the sea killed your dad early, and the sea will kill you early. I couldn't handle that, David, and I'm not even going to try." And having come this far, she could only continue to the dreaded conclusion. "I'm returning to that other world and to that other life where there is more, David, to begin again. And your son is going with me, so when the time comes he will have a choice. He will be at my mom's, and you can see him if you ever want to. I'm going back to college this spring. But I never want to see you again, David!" Ending with the hot tears of bitterness.

"But you could only rage, "No!" in disbelief, though still rigid in your own righteousness. "Mary! Then again, "Mary!"

'And that night you were again in the lounge down at Capt. Charlie's and in the crowded three deep seated and standing crowd at the long cedar bar, and you were oh hell look out mean drunk, and so scowlingly brooding that the other captains were giving you hard quick glances, then shrugging questioningly among themselves wondering what was the matter with David. And when the bullrake clammer pronounced loud and braggingly to all near and far that a man had to have more hair on his balls to pull a bullrake all day than to work the pussy ass end of a silly trawler, and you hit him a short shot chopping bloody blow with your brutalized fist straight into his lying god damn mouth, then all the captains, staggered and briefly dazed and spitting blood bullraker included, grabbed you standing there and held you vise like with twenty strong hands and arms until finally winded and exhausted you stopped flailing and then struggling, while all the time they were urging you in low forced hoarse whisper to, "cool it, Captain, cool it, we don't need the cops here, you're the original iceman, David, so cool it, kick back and relax, just kick back, Captain, relax." Then, sometime later probably much later, but maybe not, you don't remember, all of you drunken captains were packed noisily and jostlingly into the wide galley of the long line boat lashed to the dock and clear jars of finely beaded moonshine appeared from somewhere and were making their slopping over wet rounds as beer and cigarettes were doing nicely for chasers, until the last thing that you remember was bear hugging tightly the bloody mouthed bullraker as the both of you swore that you loved truly the other and that you were true brothers and that you would stick together always no matter what and to the absolute end. And it was smashed faced utterless Oscar who came spasming his wobbly way that morning and got you from somewhere amid the littered heap of passed out captains who were sprawled all entwined and snoring thickly and foul breathedly throughout the wide galley on the deck on their backs and on their stomachs and on their sides and on as well as under the shoved around tables and the seats with the group picture of you all looking like a farmer had sowed drunk seeds and now the crop was ready for harvest, and led you little boy lost and being returned like down the dock and to the lashed Evening Star. And it was our Oscar who fed you hot soup and hot coffee by the steaming burning spoonful but you could only sit stunned and hurting badly from several pains, with one being physical and the other being emotional, in your captain's chair before the wheel and stare out like an adrift forever now and always lonely soul and across this earlier herself's proud bow. And it was our Oscar, himself, who single-handedly cast off herself and got underway and managed the wandering channel and then took herself outbound with you included across the treacherous bar and through the inlet and out to sea once again. And it was only after months of living onboard Evening Star, when you were home, before you could return to live in the silent white frame house with the green shutters on Elm Street, that had the open field in front that overlooked the dry docked boats and the boat railway and the wood dock and the deep channel that wanders so.

'But you were tender with Mary,' he thought. 'And you do know that. If only tender sometimes, and if only tender in your own way.'

"Yes, tender sometimes," he said outloud. "And tender in my own way. But it was not enough. Was it? Not nearly enough."

'No, it was not nearly enough. At least not for Mary's needs. But it was the most that you could do, and that's all that you could expect of yourself.'

"But she was a pure joy, and a sure comfort to me. And certainly the finest thing ever in my life."

'Yes, clearly she was all those things. And one more. She was a sea anchor also. So that never again would you drift without a home.'

"And my son! Lord, a man is not living when he is without a son," he said, as his anguish grew, and brought with it the sore return of the personal pain.

'Yes, there is also our precious young David. A man and a son and a man and a wife, are truly equal treasures to cherish.'

"Had I not lost Mary, then I would not have lost young David," he said, seeing it all completely, and in its simplest perspective. "And could not the loss of Mary have been prevented? Had I been more tender toward her, and more often, then the loss of Mary could have been prevented."

'Possibly so, yes, and probably so. But not necessarily so. There just is not any way of knowing that now for sure. That is speculation, speculation after the fact, just as so much in life and in living is speculation after the fact.'

"But to know that I will never again lie with my Mary, in the way that I did., And to know that I will never again hold my son, in the way that I did," he said, as his anguish now became grim pain indeed. "Lord, those are bitter things to accept."

'Yes, bitter, bitter things they are to accept, and worse. Because you must learn to live with them also. And the pain of them will never change, the pain of them will never lessen. But you did give tenderness to the full extent that you could give tenderness. And to a different Mary, this extent may have been sufficient. But then that is speculation once again. Our Mary just had larger requirements, only that. And you simply could not fulfill her larger requirements, not and still meet all the many other requirements that are within your wide and heavy responsibility. Because to live and to work daily year after year as a commercial fishing captain is to have many many requirements to fulfill. And these requirements, absolute demands, even, are unique among all the different types of work that men choose to do.'

"Yes the unique demands of this my work are great indeed. And the daily strain and the daily drain that these demands have are great and unique also," he said, as now he could begin to see it all with a broader and less personal perspective."

'Because in no other work must the man, the captain, contend with so many variables, so many obstacles, and so many fluctuations. And surmount these, all of them, though they are in constant change. Most of which are merely harmful, others of which are just dangerous, but some of which are truly hostile.'

"Yes, a man in a boat upon the sea is a far different and a far more serious a matter than a man in a tractor upon the land, or a man at a machine in a building, or even a man at an airplane's controls in the air. Harm and danger are always present in every type of work, to varying degrees. But only in a boat upon the sea is there actual and true hostility present. Hostility that must be contended with and surmounted daily and year after year," he said, as now his perspective had become universal.

'That is it exactly,' he thought. 'Because at no other workplace can insignificant things so suddenly and so completely loom and then become critical things, life threatening things. And this is the only workplace where that which a man has to give must be so measured and so portioned, and so gradually and so evenly distributed. This is true. And Mary's portion just was not sufficient for her needs. But that was the largest portion that you could give to her, and still have enough to go around to the everything and to the everyone that requires a daily portion. While at the same time being absolutely positive that the reserve is maintained. It is this reserve that cannot be tapped. Not tapped for anything, not tapped for anyone, not even for Mary. Because just as surely as you tap it once, even for good reason, you will tap it again and then again, for any reason. And then when the sea presents the cruel bill for her emergency portion that is due and payable fully and upon demand suddenly and immediately in a truly hostile real sea crisis. Then and woe unto you and yours, your reserve will have been tapped out. The account overdrawn. Because as the captain you are the small god over your small world, and you are responsible in it and for it totally. And to whatever end there may be. So it is the reserve that must be guarded jealously, religiously even, and very diligently maintained, even at the expense of all and everything else. Because the sea, ah, she does certainly stalk endlessly the weak and the unprepared.'

"But what a terrible terrible price for a man to have to pay," he said, quickly returning the conversation to the simplest of personal perspectives.

'Yes. Indeed a terrible terrible price. For you, and for all captains. But the choice remains, and will so. Continue paying, or close the account. One, or the other. Though once a captain, as they say, always a captain.'

"Then it is a dilemma based upon the priorities."

'No. It is a decision based upon what is foremost.'

"But to know that I will never again lie with my Mary, in the way that I did. And to know that I will never again hold my son, in the way that I did," he said, as again the anguish became grim sore pain.

'Indeed, a terrible terrible price,' he thought.

And it was.

And here off shore and getting farther and farther from it steadily now with the passing of time, the sea breeze that rose every evening every spring at around nine o'clock to blow away the overland haze and to cool the land there, that is the same one that did rise once again a while ago and did come up suddenly from only a point or two off Bright Dawn's proud bow, and with it, this same already arisen sea breeze, the sea swells did rise suddenly also from just barely swells to two to four foot swells, and with that then a loud whisper rustling wind clatter song did also set in there in earnest there among the steel cables and the lines and the ropes that so maze shrouded the lowered and locked horizontal abeam opposing iron outriggers. And this strange singing song of steel against steel twanging and steel against iron clanging and rope against anything thudding was a rippling and a vibrating and a strummed, even haunted, song of pale enchantment. And the already arisen sea breeze did also seize quickly the twin diesel exhaust that gushed now spewing thickly from the two small barrel size mufflers gaped mouthed tailpipes, and this so seized exhaust did then trail aft and off into two separate and two sea breeze scattered thin streamers that were then quickly left behind here in this night of the soon rising sliver moon and the already many bright stars with soon to be more, as herself with himself included did continue to progress outbound progressing and getting further offshore steadily still into that which is named Onslow Bay that is, yet is not, a Bay for previously stated reasons. And the already arisen sea breeze did then cause yet another something to occur, as it did create upon the corrugated sea a gradually increasing self inertia momentum, also of the seas own already swelled surface. And because of this inertia momentum the already sea swells did then increase themselves and gradually higher still to five to seven foot swells, that while these would surely cause belly turning queasy discomfort to a dry lander, they still were not the bad rolling and the hard pitching comber swells that would demand, command even, himself's undivided attention to herself's course and stability. Though this point was rapidly approaching, and would in fact arrive soon if this inertia momentum continued to increase, and therefore did cause these swells to increase again upon themselves to higher still higher. As himself wisely and routinely and from long sea experience did now at least begin to give a bit more attention to this herself's navigation. Because now in addition to himself's considering the wind velocity and direction and the current velocity and direction, these much higher footed swells had begun to cause yet another, and this one a final something, and it was a shear effect as the force created by the higher and therefore heavier swells did begin to cause a veering off result, as each repeating then repeating then repeating bulky swell shove did push against herself at an angle, and this shearing effect of the veering result, like a crab that travels forward a little sideways, must be considered also by himself if the truly correct navigation of herself is to be achieved. Now as the so steady progress is progressing toward that chart plot point that is thirty five nautical miles offshore and is midway between Bogue Inlet and New River Inlet, and is the same point that is namely seventy seven and a quarter and thirty four and a half for those who have definite reason for going there, and is a known well invisible place here in himself's front yard.

'You had only the compass and your dead reckoning for navigation, and dead reckoning alone for catch finding, onboard Evening Star for the hundreds of searuns that you made with her,' he thinks, as he looks at the wide array of switched-off electronic boxes that are well spaced within easy forward reach about the console. 'So, captain, you can certainly compass and reckon your course on this searun tonight. But that was back when captains went to sea in trawlers. And before technicians began to go to sea in trawlers. But you can be called a technician now too. And that fits as well as captain does. Although captain you always are, and technician you only are sometimes. And profitable searuns back then came from instincts and long sea experience. But now they come from textbooks and long classroom experience, as you have said before and will say again. And it is all so different now, but yet so little has actually changed. Except the method, the means to the end, and that is very impersonal now. Because what these boxes cannot show in pictures, they can tell in readings. And gone is never again having to be one with the sea, or one with the catch,' he thinks, and he is merely a solitary shadow before the stainless steel wheel inside the darkened wheelhouse here perched atop this lonesome progressing Bright Dawn and surrounded by the high swelled and the black vast sea.

'But at the proper time young David could accept as natural this new world of scopes and screens and recorders. As naturally as you accepted the compass and reckoning and diesels. But you feel now as the sail trawler captain must have felt several generations ago, when competition forced him to discard his sails and install a gasoline engine. Something important was gained, but something important was lost also. And the sail captain never really got both feet into the engine world. Just as you will never really get both feet into this electronics world. Because it is too radical, just as the engine was too radical.

'But then Mary will see to it that young David never works on board a trawler. Because she got her fill for a lifetime of the real

48

commercial fishing. And the real commercial fisherman. And it only took her two years. But it is okay if he never does. Because trawling is no longer the simple work that it once was. Nor can it ever return to being that same simple work again. The simple work that so attracted the sons of trawling fathers. Because it can only be a suspended something now. Just as you can only be a suspended something now. With the two of you, trawling and captain, caught in this floating free middle. Two almost but not quite that have had their destinies taken from them and therefore can neither go forward or go back on their own. Because the heavy outside pressures of politics and finance have now begun to have too great an impact upon us. Like a tail that has begun to wag the dog. And this can only worsen as it continues. And gradually the dog will become only a wagless tail. And the tail will become the wagging dog. Until finally this reversed creation will be complete. Then a strange new animal will have been evolved where no such weird animal had existed before. And then this once simple work, that is no longer simple now, will be nevermore simple. And the creators of this new animal will have been the federal man and his federal brothers who will follow him. These faceless experimenters who know better. But who do not choose to do better, for their own selfish reasons. And it was you, David, who they chose to experiment upon first.

'But even such faceless theys as these with their heavy pressure impacts will not be able to change the constant fact that trawling will always be a work of daily extremes' , he thinks, as the first himself , the outloud and apparent himself, only listens quietly and does not join in this long expounding conversation of the more deeply recessed second himself.   'Because we are either blazing hot. or we are freezing cold.   We are either doing absolutely nothing. Or we cannot hustle fast enough to even keep up. It is either black night. Or it is blinding day. The catch price is either far too high, and cannot continue for long. or the catch price is far too low, and continues endlessly.   The myriad gear either works flawlessly.   Or nothing at all will keep the myriad gear working. There is either no danger anywhere.   Or there is danger everywhere. We either catch a ton. or we catch only a bucket full. The wind is either dead calm. or the wind is blowing a gale. So it is quite natural that the we who do this extremes work also become extremes ourselves. And the daily contrast in us is as great as the daily contrast is great in trawling. Because from men who are too long active. We become men who are too long idle. From men who are too long sober. We become men who are too long drunk. From men who are too long talkative. We become men who are too long silent.   From men who are too long responsible. We become men who are too long irresponsible.   And just as the contrast in trawling is very punishing on the we who are off shore. The contrast in us is also very punishing on those who wait for us on shore.

And Mary, who waited for me, endured the punishment of my contrasts for two years. And finally she had had her fill of it all for a lifetime. Then she simply took up young David and together

50

they returned to her other life that she had had before me. The life that was nice. Because Mary had choices that she could choose from. And she would see to it that young David also had choices to choose from when the proper time came for him to make them. But I was left with only that I was all alone once again in the green shuttered house that overlooks the railway. And that it was a day of warm rain when she came. And that it was a day of cold rain when she went. And that being a trawler captain was all I have ever known. Just as it had been for my father and his father and his father here in this village that is so near to the sea. And Mary was raised here also. But her family had always been dry landers. Because they preferred the nice routine that is in storekeeping. And by our marriage, Mary had become half of a high tider. But that much in name only. And on a trial basis only. Because we full high tiders, men as well as women, at least those few of us that the encroaching world has not liberated and enticed away, continue to be very obsessed with our closed lives here so near to the sea. And this is not something that we take lightly. Nor is it something that we share openly with dry landers. My mom is a full high tider. But she did not share any of being a full high tider with Mary. Not really. Because Mary was only half of a high tider. And that much only by marriage. And in name only. And on a trial basis only. But Mary misinterpreted Mom's closedness toward her as being a dissatisfaction in Mom about her high tide life. But Mom was only dissatisfied with Mary as my wife and as the mother of my son. Because all my life Mom has told me repeatedly to always avoid dry landers. To just stare blankly back at them when they speak while passing me on the streets. That dry landers cannot be trusted. Because they are not like us. And because they are not like us, they can never become like us. Not even if they try until the coming of their death rattle. Mom is a high tider indeed.

'So Mary could never have become like us. Even if she had tried until her

rattle came. But Mary had been raised liberated from this obsession with the

sea. But the influence that it had on us was total. But this was not something

that Mary understood. And she recognized it only vaguely, and she could define it not at all. But we could define this our obsession precisely. Because the sea gives and the sea takes away. And the sea always has and the sea always would. And she is us and we are she. And such basic reasoning as this has long been known well by us. So it was not necessary to entice Mary away from such a total obsession. And when her fill for a lifetime did arrive, she quickly fled from it and from us and from me with young David, and was sadder by far for her brief journey into that which she could never be, or understand.

'And it was the summer after that winter that they went quickly from me that the tourists, who had been visiting our village innocently for years without so much as a ripple, were joined by the vacationers who bought their way into here with much inland money, and then settled in to stay, who then began the real serious erosion. And their encroachment grew rapidly with the urgency of a humped swell, that became a capped wave, that became a curled comber, that smashed sprawlingly upon our once so isolated sandy shore. And after that it was no longer possible for us few remaining high tiders to avoid dry landers, whether villagers or tourists or vacationers. Nor would we ever again be able to escape from them.

'And the first of the vacationers to arrive were the Daisys, the very beautiful temptresses, who appeared suddenly with the completion of the side by side high glass condominium complexes, that were so suddenly completed out on the ocean front at Emerald Isle up from Bogue Inlet, and where the wind gnarled ancient fir tree dune covering had been thoroughly bulldozed a thousand yards wide and a mile long and then burned from existence.

But these Daisys had been long and deeply liberated. And the liberation that they practiced was a very sophisticated form of liberation, and the liberation of professionals. So Mary could never be as liberatedly advanced as they. But the Daisys would never be even vaguely aware of our obsession with the sea. While Mary was at least vaguely aware of it. But could the Daisys have been even vaguely aware of our obsession, they would have cared about it even less than Mary had cared about it. Because the Daisys are always too completely self controlled and too reserved to allow themselves to ever submit to being in the obligating position of being enticed either to or entice from anything or anyone. Because never being truly personal is vital to their sophistication. Because being truly personal toward anything or anyone does not have a place in their professional liberationism. So the Daisys could not be truly personally affected, as they calmly observed our vast sea from the high distance of their cooled and their dimmed condos, that overlooked so grandly our tumbling sandy shore that was below and away in both directions stunningly and to the haze of the horizon. But the Daisys did announce that our village was quaint. And that the villagers were quaint. And that we high tiders were quaint also. And then they quickly telephoned their many far inland Daisy friends and told them of these their new discoveries. And they urged them all to hurry and come down here to see us high tiders and the villagers and our village before we three passed forever into yesterday. So more Daisys did arrive. Then still more Daisys arrive. And when congregated so, the Daisys were like so many pretty dolls placed upon a glass turntable. And since the mobility to come and to go swiftly is also vital to them, they were continually replacing themselves with other equally pretty dolls, that came and went swiftly also as their glass turntable slowly revolved. Because these Daisys were vacationing wives. And their grand condos and our quaint village and Capt. Charlie's have now become a newly different and exciting retreat, for their shorter vacations during the summer, from their one long vacation that lasted for the remainder of the year there far inland.

'Daisy has children who are well behaved. And Daisy has a husband who is well behaved also. And success is as vital to Daisy as is mobility vital. So her husband is as distinguished as she is

54

pretty. And he flies in in his private plane on Fridays. And he flies out in his private plane on Sundays. And Daisy and her husband and her children are a nice family. And they are all well behaved. And Daisy would not have it any other way. But nothing truly personal though. Because the ever present nothing truly personal is as vital to Daisy as is being well behaved. And for the four evenings each week of her shorter summer vacation, from Mondays until Thursdays, she came together with the many other pretty Daisy dolls at Capt. Charlie's for a fine leisurely seafood meal with much good wine.

'Then with their fine seafood leisurely meals over, they went by twos and threes laughing and chatting together familiarly from the well lighted dining room into the less lighted foyer, where the heavy wood entrance doors are, and then through the small swinging doors that leads into the barely lighted lounge, where they reshuffled themselves into threes and fours and settled into the tables that are out from the raised bandstand, and ordered more good wine. Ready talk for friend or stranger, that is relaxed and interesting and correct and captivating, is as vital to the Daisys as are all the other vitals. And after their much good wine, we high tiders became beyond quaint and into fascinating to them. We captains, who were there lined three deep seated and standing at the long cedar bar. And this was as close as they had ever allowed themselves to come to the quick stronger danger that is always present in very different men who are obsessed. Men who are too truly personal. Men who are neither liberated nor successful nor well behaved nor mobile. Men who are the extremes that men become because of the sea. And every evening every week from Mondays until Thursdays, during that summer, the threes and fours table seated Daisys that were there in the lounge, became very excited by the close danger presence of such extreme men as we. And we captains could smell the musty smell of their excitement on their breaths, along with the much good wine. And we could see their excitement in their excited eyes that shone flashingly there in the barely lightedness. And we could feel their excitement in their delicately cupped hands that trembled excitedly against our brutalized hands as we lit their thin cigarettes. And then we knew that between their legs, that was usually cool and dry and forbidding, was now warm and wet and ready. So we captains struck as would sharks striking small schools of bluefish. But bedding with Daisy is for her medicinal purposes only. And it is for her sex rather than for our lovemaking. And Daisy will not have it any other way. And it is nothing truly personal of course. Because Daisy is a bluefish like no bluefish a shark has ever struck before. And afterwards it was us captains who felt used and then discarded. And then very few of us ever bedded with a Daisy again. Because to do so regularly would mean for the captor to somehow strangely become the captive. But they had arrived. The Daisys had arrived. And they had bought in here to stay, with their powerful inlander money. So our sandy seashore already was theirs. And soon our quaint village would be theirs also. And there was no escape. Because never again could they be avoided. And the day the Daisys first arrived, was the day that the village and the villagers and we high tiders began quickly to pass forever into yesterday.

'And that was the summer that the federal man arrived also,' he thought here in this night of the sliver moon and the now many stars, as Bright Dawn trembled herself still, into and out of the heavy swelled swells with their shoving shear effect, and rumbled herself slightly still, from the massive potential power that the below twin diesels contain there ready, that is unleashed fully and massively when trawling herself Is two huge scooping trawl nets, and when the weather builds and becomes quite foul and this full massive power is necessary for proper stability amid the seawater that slides and hisses and is mountainous and blowing.

'But of the two arrivals that summer, his arrival was the most destructive,' he thought on. 'For sure. For sure. At least to me. Because the Daisys spread their destruction evenly around and steadily upon everyone like a bad fog. But the federal man concentrated his destruction directly and upon me alone like a single evil ramming by a large dark shoal. But at first he had offered such grand promise and such great hope. But then these became disillusionment and bankruptcy, like the sudden up then down ride of a runaway roller coaster. For sure. And finally to end here and now with this searun tonight. Indeed.

'But it with him had begun simply enough, while we had Evening Star high and dry and naked embarrassed looking out of water. With Oscar dead red lead paint dusty from bottom scraping.

And me bilge grime greasy from engine overhauling. And the federal man expensive suited uncertain there at the hatch opening looking down at me.'

"Are you David Midgett?"

But I didn't look at him.

"Are you David Midgett!?"

But I still didn't look at him.

"Hello down there! Are you David Midgett!?"

Then I looked blankly at him just as Mom had said to always look at inlanders.

"Are you David Midgett?"

But I returned to engine overhauling.

"The fellow at the office over there said he thought David Midgett was working in the hole of this ship."

"Below." I said.

"Below?"

"Not down there."

"Below."

"Boat." I said.

"Boat?" He asked.

"Not ship."

"Boat."

Then I pointed aft without looking.

"Is he back there?"

"Hold."

"Hold?"

"Not hole."

"Hold."

Then I look blankly at him again.

"Aft." I said.

"Aft?" he asked.

"Not back there."

"Aft."

But I didn't say anything.

"Is he aft?"

"No. The hold is aft."

"Well, where is David Midgett?"

"Engine compartment."

"Where's that?"

"You're looking at it."

"Then you're David Midgett."

But I only continued to look blankly at him.

"You are. Aren't you."

"Why do you want him."

"He's the best trawler captain along the coast."

"You got that right."

"I'm going to help him get a modern new trawler."

"Does he know that?"

"No. Not yet."

"Why would he want one?"

"We're going to update and expand our commercial fishing fleet."

"We are?"

"The CFD slash DOC is."

"They are?"

"Yes, we are."

"Why?"

"To better compete internationally. It's an increased trade, balance of payments, world food shortage, sort of thing. Our boats are thirty years behind the Russian and Japanese boats."

"Ships." I said.

"Ships?" he asked.

"They have ships."

"Exactly!"

But I only looked blankly at him.

"Say. Are you David Midgett? You are. Aren't you?"

CHAPTER THREE

When the long long new earth spinning top whirling and gathering and compressing had slowed. When the long long groaning of the splitting seamed and the colliding plated earth crust had stilled and had faded. When the long long speeding of the roaring debris wind had churned and had rearranged and had swept and then had eased and had gone on by. When the resultant long long silence then was unending even at its ending. When the long long tearing of the moaning jagged sudden ice had lingered and had stalled and had receded. When the long long violent sea had pounded itself so frantically into submission upon the high peaked shore, and then had so gradually fallen back while grumbling still, to splash upon the far and the flatter sandy shore. When the long long transformations of the sea squirt began to evolve into all that would root and entwine and attach upon this bare raw land. When the long long wait itself waited. When the weeds then grew to forty foot heights only to space dust sunlessness die into crashing crushing layers of the peat that would compact hotly into the coal. When the long long whirring of the insects finally was chorused by the awkward croaking of the first hesitant frogs. When hairy almost men could only stoop and cower and slobber and hide. Then the brilliant foliage that was so very long in the coming came, and in abounding vast tangles to color the land. And the singing winged swarms that were so very long in the coming came, and in abounding sweeps to cheer the cloudy low sky. And the quick finned schools that were so very long in coming came, and in abounding swirls to sparkle beneath the rippled white water surface. And the long long contract that the rivers would have with the sea was begun, as unbreechable and as forever endurable. And the long long wait waited still.

Then the upright men that were so very long in the coming came, and by several they curiously traveled the healthful rivers reverently in burn hollowed tree trunks. But then, and at last, oddly clothed men came also. And they came in the groups that would soon become the crowds, that then would soon become the abounding masses. Because the long long trust experiment that was so very long in the coming had come. It had arrived. And it would continue and it would develop and it would unfold, now in racing multiples of man activity.   But strangely it became immediately necessary, imperative even, for these oddly clothed men to begin giving new names to huge portions of land. New names that would soon become rigid domain lines upon a boundary chart. Because they knew something that only they knew. And when these men had come sufficiently, they even gave new names to their trails and to their crossroads and to their locales. Then new names also to the sounds and to the shores and to the swamps and to the plains and to the hollows and to the mountains and to the rivers. Because they knew something that only they knew.

But the Flat River and the Tar River already had long long

endured the unbreechable contract that they had long long had with the sea. Because they both begin in the high hill rolling valley country near Roxboro in Person County in North Carolina, where the hard rains trickle down red clay banks and over pebbles and around rocks as it congregates itself into moving fingerlets, that gather themselves into branches, that then join other branches, that converge themselves into the streams, and then into the creeks, that converge finally into these two separate newly named but ancient rivers. A huge land drainage system having long long ago begun. And when the Flat River has collected itself broad and shiny at Lake Michie, it then courses itself along and on down until the fork above Durham where it embraces to itself the eastward coursing from Hillsborough, Eno River. But once united with the Eno, the Flat River suddenly loses its past identity for no particular reason. And it becomes the swifter coursing Neuse River, that bends and wanders southward mostly past Raleigh, that east west compromise city that finally did become the capital. Meanwhile the Tar River courses itself along and on down for a long ways secure in its own complete identity, as it gathers creeks and wanders and gathers creeks and wanders, until then dramatically horseshoeing itself northward then eastward briefly then southward past Rocky Mount, that old railroad and tobacco city. But when the Tar River has coursed itself past Greenville, it suddenly becomes the Pamplico River for no particular reason. And when the Pamplico River courses itself past the original Washington, it is wide and deep. Meanwhile the Neuse River shallows itself and rapids itself for a ways as it courses itself past its own producing sheer cliffs, that are below Goldsboro, where it then dramatically becomes wide and deep itself also, as it courses itself past Kinston, but then and then only briefly cannot quite decide its true direction until it courses itself truly finally then past New Bern, that colonial city. But having coursed past New Bern, the Neuse River then and suddenly loses its identity to the enormity that is the Pamplico Sound. And for the same good particular reason that a thick finger yields its lesser identity to the larger identity of a huge hand. But not before the Neuse River has embraced to itself the Bay River. And once the Pamplico River has embraced to itself the Pango River, then suddenly it also loses its identity, and for the same good particular reason, to the enormity that is the Pamplico Sound.

The Pamplico Sound, that is land locked far seaward by the Core Banks, except for several inlets from Cape Lookout to Cape Hatteras to Nags Head. This enormous Pamplico Sound that has long long abounded with the myriad life that has always been so land and sound and sky abundant, because of the long long unbreechably enduring contract that it has had with the high hilled Flat River and the rolling valleyed Tar River. But the clams long long homed in the sandy bottom at Portsmouth Island are now tainted, because of the crankcase oil that was spilled at Roxboro.

"A million dollars!!!" The one brother said in sudden disbelief.

And the other brother could only look down self-consciously. Then smile a little defensive smile. "But she'll be right, Harold."

"She sure as hell should be, David."

64

"She'll be the best trawler anywhere around here. Several of her sisters are trawling out of Marathon, Florida. And several out of Gloucester. But none in between. She'll be the first." He said as anticipated large pride in the new trawler replaced the moment of defensive self-consciousness because of the staggering price.

"But a million dollar mortgage! David, David, David." This last shaking his head slowly as pessimism began to replace the disbelief.

"Half of that is for her electronics. She'll be super advanced, Harold. Something from the future. And the federal man says the mortgage is manageable. So the government is behind me on it with the bank."

"But dad would have mortgaged mom before mortgaging his trawler. And he wouldn't have mortgaged mom until the tide never changed again."

"But that was back when commercial fishermen were still considered next to worthless. And banks wouldn't even talk with us, much less the government. Now the government is behind us, just as they have always been behind the land farmers. We're farmers of the sea now. And our crops are finally as valuable as the land crops."

"Well, that's progress at least. Whether it's for the good or for the bad though only time will tell. And I guess you have to join that progress, David. But a million dollar mortgage." Shaking his head slowly again as full doubt replaced just pessimism.

"I can either join it, or get shoved aside and buried by it,

Harold."

"Wonder how dad would have felt about it?"

"He would have hollered and fumed about any mortgage and all inlanders for a week. Then agreed that I have to take this opportunity, and take the gamble that goes along with it. If I don't they'll just find another captain."

"Yeah, you're right. Dad was always hardheaded, but eventually he was realistic too."

"Why don't you come in with me! Dad died wanting us together on a trawler. It'll be like when we were boys with dad on Evening Star. And Bright Dawn is plenty big enough, and plenty complicated enough. Just you and me and Oscar."

"No, David. When I left home before dad died, I said I would return to visit, but never again to trawl. And that still goes. I don't love the sea. And I don't ever want to be seasick again."

"Harold, all of us captains have a love-hate thing with the sea. And we get seasick too. Even dad did when the swells got that certain bucking rhythm along with the rolling and the pitching."

"No. Trawling just isn't important to me. And it never was. And the gamble is already too great. The catches aren't always where you think they will be. Or in the poundage that you think they will be. And some years the catches don't even come at all. No, David. The gamble is already too great. And this million dollar mortgage you're assuming on top of everything else is absolutely unbelievable."

"But the federal man says it's manageable, Harold. And the

government is behind me on it."

"Well, I just hope that they are still behind you if you ever need them."

The chain sawed-on a ragged angle stumps of the so very old yard trees there in the cold and the dark and the muck are all that remains of the two hundred farms that now are flooded by twenty five feet of water at the deepest depth for the three thousand acres that surrounds here like a big teardrop that is widely margined by scraped raw land that is grass seeded. The long curved concrete dam reservoirs all of this water into obedience for the upon demand use of the City of Wilson and the City of Rocky Mount that are in opposite directions with one south and the other north from it by a nearly equal number of miles. And the buried intakes that come from their separate water treatment plants to this big teardrop reservoir are like gigantic straws that supply fluid to two sprawling giants by plastic veins that run unseen beneath thick idle topsoil that has always been rich and black and productive. But the Tar River is harnessed now and so it shivers and it can only struggle to rush frantically over the electrically adjustable spillways of the hard dam. Because the long long enduringly unbreechable contract that it has long long had with the Pamplico Sound is impeded. But the two brothers are aways down river past several slow ess bends and they cannot see the Tar River frantic shiver struggle against its impediment from this their another world removed world. And the afternoon shade that the high hardwood trees provide is pleasant after the harsh glare of midday. But

December is near and December is coming. And the two brothers are seated with legs out-stretched in side by side lounge chairs on the long brick patio that is behind a large brick house. They talk easily together and they hear the come and go of the breeze in the soon to be turning burnt leaves of the high trees. The chopped stalks of the recently swing bladed undergrowth show as stark white dot clusters on the steep bank that quickly slopes to where the Tar River here is dirty brown narrow and deep. And from above and beyond it, the two brothers can see the tree branch splintered shadows that the come and go breeze moves upon the dusty water surface. But December is near and December is coming And the shrimp fry that nurseryed in the endless marshes at Swan Quarter died from the thick silt that ran from an eroded field near Louisburg.

"Why wouldn't the government still stand behind me if I need them, Harold?"

"Because anything can go wrong, David. Anything! And everything can go wrong. It has before in trawling, several times over the years. And it can again."

"But we're in this together for the long run. That's what the federal man says."

"I hope he means it."

"Well of course he means it!" Dismissing the doubt quickly as something so obviously remote that it was not even worth discussing.

"Okay, David." The one brother said after having raised all the doubts that so concerned him. While knowing that the other brother was hardheaded just as their dad had been hardheaded. And knowing too that eventually he would be realistic also. "When will Bright Dawn be completed?"

"A week, ten days. Not long. They'll phone. I was in St. Augustine last month for her launching. She's a true beauty for sure. They're trimming her out now, and installing her electronics. I'll be down for a week of sea trials and instrument training. Then I'll bring her up for the last of the brown shrimp run out of the inlets as they start south for the winter."

"You'll bring her up the Inland Waterway though."

"No. Bluewater her all the way."

"Good lord, David, why?! When it isn't necessary."

"There's bound to be a hard squall somewhere along the way. May as well find out whether she'll float. And how she handles in weather."

The one brother is completely at ease with the close tall surroundings here this far inland and at home secure and comfortable. But the other brother is restless here where his squinted vision for sun screening far seeing is so limited by dense hardwood forest and its tangled undergrowth that is near and there just beyond the river.

"Keep daring her, David. Keep daring her. "As a frown of concern comes again to his forehead in deep crossing wrinkles.

"That's where I work, Harold. You have a workplace. Well, bluewater is my workplace."

"But there's a big big difference! And you know there is."

"Of course there is. But working at sea every day becomes as routine as all other workplaces become everyday routine."

"But your approach is so fatalistic. Always daring her unpredictable worst even when it isn't necessary."

"I'm at my workplace and doing my job, Harold. Not daring her. And I'm realistic, not fatalistic. Since the sea is never predictable, the sea is always predictable. Since she's never the same, she's always the same."

"It isn't that simple. And you do dare her. You know you do. Just as dad dared her."

"Well, she will either serve or kill. That goes with the territory."

"She killed dad."

"No. Dad killed dad. He knew better than to bother with a harmless loose stern rope when we were taking rollers across us the way we were. She just happened to be the means."

"No. Dad loved her. And she betrayed him."

"No, dammit Harold. Since she always betrays, she never betrays. Dad knew that."

"That's fatalism, David."

"No, it's realism."

"It isn't. But if it were, why couldn't you have some of that realism about this mortgage of yours?"

"We've already talked about the mortgage, Harold. Now you're comparing apples with oranges. One doesn't have anything to do with the other."

"But there is something bad wrong about that mortgage. It's too sudden, and it's too easy."

"Or it's the best opportunity I'll ever have offered to me."

"No, something's bad wrong about it. Most of all a million dollars is too damn much."

"But I have to take the gamble. If I don't another captain will, like I said. And the potential that Bright Dawn represents is too great to pass up, Harold."

"But at least don't bluewater her bringing her up. That really isn't necessary."

"That's what she's built for. And if she can't handle it I better know it before I start trawling her. There are enough surprises then without adding another surprise."

"Keep daring the sea, David. Keep daring her. You're even hoping for a hard squall. And the worse, the squall, the better you'll like it."

"Like I said, she will either serve me or kill me." And in his mind he was already captain aboard Bright Dawn. And bluewater bringing her up, hard squall and all and whatever the hell else.

Then they are quiet together for awhile as each withdraws alone into the many things of their separate and their so very different lives. The other brother is far from home and he is restless. The one brother is at home and he is secure. The afternoon shade that the high trees provide is pleasant after the midday glare. And they can hear the come and go breeze in the leaves with December near and December coming. And they can see the splintered shadows of the branches that move upon the dusty water Tar River surface. The other brother is blonde haired blown looking with a full beard rusted to a dirtyish yellow grey with a no longer young mouth that now has gone hard and is long weathered by the brutal weather of blistering days and freezing nights and always and ever the constant wind the constant wind that has left his eyes so streaked red around blue and forever squint narrowed. But the one brother is an unweathered and unharden and an unwinded and an unbrutalized look alike copy of the all these other brother. And the one brother is a two year younger and a neater looking and a gentler looking copy of the harsher looking original older other brother. And for this awhile they are quiet together. But the sea turtle hatchlings that broke sand in a mass scampering from among the sea grassed dunes at Avon wandered wrong way panically upon the asphalt road and were mass tire smashed because the lights from the beach cottages disoriented their night horizon sightings for their run trek to the safer surf.

"That's exactly the attitude I had to get away from." The one brother said as suddenly he spoke his deep thinking thoughts. And the outloud sound of his voice started him.

And the other brother's squint narrow eyes widened in surprise for a moment because of the abrupt end to their silence. Then he said, "What attitude, Harold?"

And already having begun, the other brother could only continue. "That whole selfrighteous, 'she'll serve me or kill me, ' attitude, David, that you and all the high tiders have down home. That even I had for awhile. That your work and your lives makes you larger than life figures from an old romantic sea poem rather than real down to earth people."

"Harold, you know that it's a hard life. And that only hard people can live it. Very single minded people too, Harold. Independent. Fierce even. And you know that too. " And the other brother's eyes were squint narrow once again as now he looked steadily at the one brother.

"That's exactly the attitude, David. Just more of it. "

But the other brother did not reply yet as he continued to look steadily at the one brother. As he then began to realize that a buried basic big difference now existed between them.

"That whole damn attitude that you high tiders are a special people. Larger than life people because of your three hundred year isolation with the sea. And so chosen that even today you still feel it is your duty to appear dumb and be rude to all inlanders. This in a selfish attempt to keep them outside your lives and away from your village as though they were a dreaded disease about to infect something sacred."

But the other brother could not take seriously this talk from the one brother. And as he turned his steady look away, he began to look just restless once again at the below and beyond river. Then his long weathered mouth smiled a slow good smile there surrounded by his blown looking full beard. "Yes, we did do that, Harold. You and me and the other kids when we were young. And the old folks still do it. Have always done it. And this treatment worked well until recently. But the inlanders are over running us. And they can't be stopped. So it's really useless to do it any longer."

"You still think that it's cute! Don't you? That it's funny! I did. But I don't now. And I haven't for a long time. It's small, David, and mean and conceited and backward. And what's worse even I have begun to receive that treatment. And do you know who from? Mom! My own mother! She hardly speaks to me anymore when we visit down home. And she doesn't speak to Nancy and the kids at all. That's silly. That's cruel, David! And that's ignorant."

"Hell, Harold, mom's old folks. She's from the old days, the old times. Inlanders. Anyone who didn't arrive by sea has always been distrusted. Feared even, and to be avoided no matter what. Sure it's backward and ignorant. But it's natural too. Mom's never been inland. And to her it simply doesn't exist. She probably didn't see three inlanders for the first forty years of her life. But it isn't just an attitude with mom, Harold. it's all she's ever known, and a way of life. If you aren't a fisherman, or a fisherman's family, you simply do not exist to her. She's old folks, Harold."

"But I am her son, David, and Nancy is my wife. And our kids are her grandkids."

"Harold, mom still does what high tider women have always done. She clams with her bare feet. She crabs with meat on a string. She handline fishes. She cans from her garden. And she

74

waits for dad to return from the sea. For the sea to finally give him up. That's her life. All of it, Harold. Just as it was her mom's and her mom's and her mom's. And its impenetrable. Nothing else exists for her. You do because you are her son. But only grudgingly so because you no longer are a fisherman. Nancy and the kids just don't exist at all to her. Mary did for awhile because I had taken her for my wife, a fisherman's wife. But only grudgingly so because Mom sensed that Mary would not last. I'm a fisherman, therefore I exist to Mom. And young David exists to her because as my son she's convinced that he will continue our fisherman tradition. Mom's from those old days, Harold, those old times. You should realize that. You certainly have been around it long enough."

And then as the two brothers look further down river together they can see what remains today of the rock and mortar dam after all these many years where the river makes another bend there and then goes on about its never ending journey into the hardwoods beyond. But the broken dam only tickles the river there. And it does not impede the river there. And the river plays there and tumbles there. And there the river laughs with the dam. And the fishes rest in the lazy swirls there before the dam. And they feed fat upon the tripping along bugs that break the dusty water surface there. And the long long contract that the Tar River has long long had with the Pamplico Sound remains unbroken. And the two brothers together can see the running deep water passing the sloughway where the wood paddle giant waterwheel had so long stood tall and slow turning. And this pleasant afternoon shade there peaceful is like the lonesome singing of a near and coming December song. And they can see the now loosened stones that remain of the scattered foundation walls of the old mill there sadly jumbled upon this ancient land of rich earth and undergrowth tangles.

"I've been around it too long, David. Far too long in fact. And of course I realize that mom is from the old days. The old times. But that doesn't give her the right to only grudgingly admit that I exist. Me! Her son. And that my wife and kids don't even exist at all. That's inexcusable, David! That's unheard of. And she simply doesn't have the right! No one does." And this now surfacing bitterness of sharp words and the twisted face of the one brother was painfully awkward to witness.

"But Harold, mom is mom. And you can't change her anymore than you can change the sea. Anymore than dad could be changed. Or any of the old folks for that matter. They're all impenetrable." Soothingly. Brotherly.

"But by accepting this from her, I condone it. I excuse it. I say she's right. And that I can't do. I won't do. And I don't have to be anywhere around such wrong backwardness. And I won't be, David. Not ever again." This spoken with the low and slow finality of a new decision.

But the other brother did not choose to reply. So he just continued to look further downriver to the ancient mill with his restlessness only a barely seeable presence.

"David, I've hauled around the guilt for not staying a fisherman, for not staying at home, for a lot of years. But no longer. No, no longer. Because I haven't done a thing to be guilty for. Not one thing. And if mom thinks I've betrayed something inevitable and sacred, that's her problem. And if you also think so, that's your problem. And to hell with both of you. But it is no longer my problem. And I'm through hauling the guilt for it. "

But still the other brother did not choose to reply. And in the barely seeable restlessness of his deep mind there was only the windy sea at work to confront.

"And when I leave home now after a visit, it's like leaving far behind a tired age that finally wore itself out there at land's end. And none of it, that age, its life, its people, has a relevance today."

"Well, it sure as hell does to me, Harold! And to mom! And to all of us there!" This involuntary outburst. This quick lashing slashing outburst. Then his lip biting silence again.

"David, y'all will live that same old romantic sea poem forever. And it's great for story telling time. And fine for books. But it's not relevant today."
This calmly spoken with the low and slow finality from before.

But the other brother just bit lip and cringed. And once again he remained silent. Because the bitterness of the one brother had to be spoken fully now finally. Spoken before it could ever begin to ease for him. Before it could ever begin to be released by him as a thing too heavy to continue hauling also along with quilt. Because not only had the bitterness been only wearing away at the one

77

brother like a constantly rubbing nag. But he had also begun to wear this bitterness close about himself as one would wear a harsh and a hurting cloak. A long wearing away cloak that finally should be discarded.

"The thicker sea air at home is a welcome and a wonderful change to inlanders, David. And that's the way it should be . Because it represents sunning and swimming and fishing and playtime to them. But that air chokes and stifles me. And it is musty and decayed to me. And it is the past to me. But my breathing suddenly becomes easier as soon as I start inland. Because the air is fresher and cleaner to me there. And the nearer I get to here. To these hills, to these forests, to these fields, to this river. The fresher and cleaner the air becomes. Because there's growth and there's change here, David! And mostly we like each other here. And always we love these hills. Even our congestion is exciting. And the problems that it creates are challenges. The seasons are far more distinct here. Each with its own colors and its own mood and its own dreams. The weather and the wind are surprises that are anticipated. Even the storms here bring that special thrill of huddling cozily indoors against them. They aren't dreaded and feared. And we don't run before them. Their fury may damage us, but it can't destroy us. And the tide doesn't absolutely dominate everything here. If we are sometimes intense and preoccupied, and sometime we are, it is an intense preoccupation with life. Not with death, David! All life, and a full life. We don't isolate ourselves from life here. We share it, and we belong to it.

Nancy and I enjoy each other. And we enjoy our kids. And our home, our river, our hills. Here we simply enjoy living, David! And we all grow even closer together through this living. We don't hide and pretend here. We don't drag life around like an old anchor here. And I will not feel guilty for having all of this, David! Not ever again. I simply refuse to. And I don't have anything to apologize for. Not to you. Not to mom. Not to anyone. Not even to dad when the sea ever does give him up." And having spoken so freely at last, the one brother was free at last. And gripping this newly won freedom tightly, his enthusiasm soared and it roamed.

"He'll be a crusty captain indeed when she ever does give him up." Then the other brother's laughter broke his long cringed silence. And the tension from their buried basic big difference then drifted and thinned. And it became no more than a passing cloud that has once been a fender between them.

"For sure, for sure." And the one brother laughed also. And with his laughter he reluctantly began to return from the roam and the soar of his newly freed enthusiasm. A quick spiral downward to the too solid confines of now. Himself, this one brother, an unweathered and an unhardened and an unwinded and an unbrutalized look-alike copy of the all these other brother.

"So and no otherwise, Harold, hillmen desire their hills."

"And you desire the sea, David, the sight of saltwater unbounded."

"So and no otherwise. Each side of one coin."

Then they were once again quiet together for awhile. And

the last afternoon breeze cooled. And it moved high in the hardwoods. And the everywhere shadows lengthened. But upriver the Tar River is harnessed at the hard dam. And it shivers there. And it struggles to rush frantically over the adjustable spillway there.

"Mary brought young David over for a visit last weekend. But mostly he just played alone down by the river."

"Her folks have been good about letting him stay with mom. The two of them are out on the water every day. And he's becoming quite a waterman."

"Yeah, Mary's not real thrilled about that."

"She wouldn't be.".

"But she won't stop it."

"He'll become whatever he must become. And she can have only so much control over that."

"But he needs you and Mary together, David. A home of his own."

"He can go trawling with me in several years. If he wants to, and Mary lets him."

"That isn't the same thing."

"It's the best I can do."

"But Mary will stop the trawling part."

"She can have only so much control, and for so long. Then it'll be up to him."

"She wants y'all to get back together. She visits us a lot from Greenville. She has a nice apartment near the campus.

Nancy helped her fix it up."

"She belongs up here. Fishermen can't play at being fishermen. And their wives can' t play at being their wives."

"Oh come on, David, Mary didn't play at being your wife."

"What else would you call it? She doesn't belong down home anymore than you do."

"There you go with that guilt shit again! Must you always be so one way?! Your way! The sea's way! Or no way'?! Just more of that same goddamn old tired attitude!"

"Things are the way they are, Harold. They can be shaded all different ways. But in the end they are the way they are."

"You never do give an inch! Do you, David?! Well, just keep on never giving an inch!"

The two large around and flat sided and worn deep grooved upper and lower granite grinding stones of the old mill are there yonder upon this rich earth ancient bank. And they remain still for the brothers to see. But the stones are tilted crazily there and half above ground. And they are green brown damp moldy. And they are matted vine overgrown there abandoned like soft heavy voices that speak from the past through this afternoon's now cooling shade. But December is near and December is coming. A December of a different kind. And the packed paths that the trodding people and the plodding mobs endlessly took to and from this mill remain still. But nothing will ever grow there on those raw solid trail ribbons from the past. And the tall standing wood paddle waterwheel remains only as a parts dismantled and carted away memory. And the breeze in the high branches move these soft heavy voices about like echoing whispers. The memory of the corn that was here ground into grits and into meal remains still. And the memory of the grains that were here ground into flour remains. But the Tar River as memory only also has begun its slow march beginning. As has the Neuse River as a memory only. And as has the Pamplico Sound as a memory only also begun its slow march beginning. This suddenly and this dramatically now after they have so very long endured. Because December is near and December is coming. This December of a different kind. Because at Oriental the flounder fry that nurseryed in the salt marshes there suffocated. Because what drained into the Neuse River from a manufacturing plant at Goldsboro caused an algae bloom there where the Pamplico Sound starts. And this severely withdrew oxygen from the frys' water.

"Why does everything I say bother you so, Harold?"

"Because you're hardheaded."

"No, there's more to it."

"Because I care."

"But I'm not critical of your life."

"But I'm your brother."

"And that gives you some rights. But not every right."

"I'm in the middle between you and Mary."

"Then you put yourself there."

"David, Mary needs more from life than just walking a widow's walk waiting for your return."

"You're a tool and die maker. And Nancy accepts the bad that comes with that."

"But we also have a life apart from that. And my income is steady. My hours regular. This house and land are almost paid for. Friends visit us. We visit them. Nancy takes classes at the community college. I'm commander of the local power boat squadron. We're building a corral for several horses. Next spring I'll break ground for forty acres of soybeans. Our lives are full and varied. Nothing is all consuming in them. And there's very little uncertainty."

"I'm a sea captain, Harold. I. Am. A. Sea. Captain. How many ways must I say it?"

"You're also a good engine mechanic, David. You could get a job up here. There's a hundred acre farm for sale downriver about a mile. The Tar really broadens there. The view is great. You could rebuild the farm house that overlooks it. Mary could continue college. Y'all and young David could be a real family there."

"Is the Tar broad enough there for Bright Dawn?"

"I'm serious."

"So am I, Harold."

"I promised Mary I would talk with you about it."

"You kept your promise."

"But you won't discuss it? At least consider it, David."

"I. Am. A. Sea. Captain."

"Mary knows you're up. Let me phone her to come over. Or

we'll go get her. You haven't seen her in months. She's still very pretty."

"She's where she belongs."

"At least see her. Talk with her."

"I'm going down home now. Oscar and I can take Evening Star for her last trawl tomorrow. Then I'll turn her over to the bank."

"But nothing's settled."

"Everything's settled. I'm going where I belong."

"Backward to the isolation.   Backward to the attitude."

"Back to the sea, Harold."

"Well, I don't feel guilty about leaving it."

The Tar River does begin to broaden itself a mile or so downriver. And the view there is indeed great. There where it lovingly begins to gather to itself more and then even more streams that become creeks that become branches. Like so many fond but reverse role children that gather to it along the way so that their mother may suckle from them for her nourishment. These sprawling natural myriad finger drainage arteries for the coastal plains. And once the Tar River has passed Tarboro and Greenville and Grimesland then it proceeds to broaden itself spectacularly.   And with the hills finally behind them the land flattens quickly and it becomes quite sandy.   But in the old days the old times the first people came trudging upriver.   First to the original people then beyond the original people. Herding and pushing them along also as they came. First by severals. Then by families.   But always inland and onward they came. And upward and westward to the hills and then to the mountains relentlessly. But some stopped. And some stayed. And beside the streams and beside the creeks and beside the branches and in the coves and on the bluffs of the bends of this broad but there narrowing river they cleared and they built and they planted. Then they hunted and they fished and they spun and they cured. And mostly they were self sufficient. And their generations scattered widely as generations will do. And relentlessly also. But some stopped. And some stayed even until today. But only rarely are they self sufficient now. And bacteria run off from the septic tank fields there. And the land fills seep that pretend to hide the no end tonnage of solid waste there. And chemicals run off from the plowed fields there. And swamps are filled for new land there. And rain erodes where the last forests are strip harvested there. And farm land is more valuable as development property there. And the Tar River no longer has its long long contract with the Pamplico Sound there. It having been recently voided violently. Because the priorities for the quality of life also are no longer precise there. And the white herons that must daily minnow stalk feed in nonchalant solitude there along the shallows and the flats at Belhaven are in constant angry flight because the pleasure boat people insist upon tearing about so like roaring things gone wild.

CHAPTER FOUR

"All right!!" he said full voice sturdily and in wholehearted approval and with complete satisfaction and out loud reverberatingly to himself , in the constant habit of all bluewatermen of frequently talking to themselves for the company of it for the reassurance of it while at sea always alone even though among others. All though here on this searun he is alone absolutely and once again he talks to himself, just as he long has done and now does and often will do here in this still close and this still darkened wheelhouse with herself our herself still slightly trembling from bow to stern and still heavily rumbling from down below and along there where her massive power lives. And himself our himself still flat footed planted and still spread legged braced and still only a shadow figure that is merely among all the many other shadow figures that are there and here in the wide and the all around forward glass, with herself still only a restless pale passing traveler a bare shimmering lonesome image even, here in this night of the now risen sliver moon. But an almost unfriendly sliver moon of impersonal light even, and the now so very many bright stars but far distant stars and cold almost dead stars even, as together our himself and our herself ride glide slide rolling and nosing and rising the shoving hulk humps of the twelve to fifteen foot shearing effect inertia momentumed swells one after the other after the other steadily and continuously, until after having scaled climbing and finally surmounting yet another swell height comber height even and almost then himself can see there over there it is across yonder and midway to the horizon, there it is the much, much larger by comparison freighter. Itself like an outlined sketch drawing in relief on a blackened board that has been lined filled in with yet a darker deeper black than the surrounding dark deep blacks of several shades and of various degrees of the above sky and the beneath sea that blend join each other at the horizon line, that is perceptible while being imperceptible also and at the same time like the fuzzy union border of two halves top and bottom of a picture photograph negative. As itself that itself that lonesome traveler also freighter rolls and noses and rises pale passing also, just as herself is doing all there simultaneously also, but itself the freighter is straddling spanning many hulk humped swells combers even and almost at a time, while herself rides glides slides and scales only one at the time. As itself is fast approaching, just as herself is fast approaching also thirty four and a half and seventy seven and a quarter that and this their mutual destination their secret meeting place their clandestine rendezvous, that precise yet invisible and chart only specific pencil point for those few who truly have a need to know and a definite and a valid reason for going there and here that quickly closes in on and achieves thirty five nautical miles offshore, and is in himself's now unruly once again and frequently so and usually so front yard there and here in the wide open yawning vast sameness that is Onslow Bay that is a bay yet is not a bay for previously stated reasons and is equidistant as the seasoned navigator would caliper mark it from Bogue Inlet and from New River Inlet.

With the "all right!!" being a sturdy exclamation of satisfied approval, an outloud testament of verification of certification even that the not known and the never to be known freighter captain does, yes indeed and in fact, indeed know positively where he is exactly in all of this unruly vast bay and is exactly where be had intended upon being and is there exactly when he had intended upon being there even though this where and this when has reasonable tolerances naturally because after all this is a sea voyage rather than a space voyage therefore the margin of error and of deviation are far more flexible and are far more forgiving. But by being well within these reasonable tolerances of where and of when and by not being wanderingly sloppy and by not being erratically confuse or assuming then put simply the freighter captain has his shit together and certainly knows what he is doing. Just as put simply himself, our himself, has his shit together and certainly knows what he is doing. Therefore these two forever to remain strangers are of an elite company are of a minority of two among but a few among all of the captains, so called and self appointed and self proclaimed, who presume to sea voyage as true captains though laughingly jokingly and foolishly so. So here, as this the telephone long distance confirmed and this the go between planned and this the weeks ahead prearranged secret meeting here and now is about to commence its commencement, here with these two anticipated champions here upon an expectant and a huge gaming field. And it is now like when two champions, first sight the other from afar and then fast approach and crest separate hills closingly and immediately they recognize the other as the anticipated champion they each were expecting. With one being a lonesome trawler and the other being a lonesome freighter, with both of them being on course and on location and on time, just as champions should be and would be. Then after pausing momentarily at the instant of their separate recognition of yes yes there he is, good, and a fellow professional too, good, and another true sea captain, good good, then they each begin again to close to nearer still nearer, first fast then gradually more slowly as they each continue to measure up and to size up the other all the while just as gaming champions should do and would do then they each close to quite near now but still respectfully cautiously so and wisely warily so here and now just prior to the moment when their actual coming to grips together their laying to together would take place here and now as their figuratively jostling together and sparing together has already begun to run its course. And so all that remains is their one on one and one from the other give and take rendezvous exchange, that soon now would begin and then continue until some time later when the quick parting from it the abrupt end of it would happen would take place with the transfer contest then competed the successful meeting then adjourned, when the still champion freighter captain would then continue on his way after having only slightly veered out of his way, when the still champion trawler captain would then double back in an inbound retracing of the outbound run, but with these two elite voyagers lonesome travelers still.

Because sometimes it is necessary to actually physically specifically begin to begin a thing before there can ever be a middle to the thing and then an end to the end of the thing. So our himself said a second "all right." But this second "all right" is the vocal trigger pull of calm resolve of beginning while the first "all right!!" had been an outloud exclamation of satisfied approval of contentment almost and this second "all right" would function as the starter's gun bang functions by officially starting this individual and this separate event that is distinct from yet inescapably related to all the other categorized events that when combined comprise this entire episode. Ah, but this event is the feature the goal the reason the main the purpose event of all the related events that have led to and soon would trail from this single event like supporting building blocks like stair steps to and from. Because this event now is the transfer of the goods at sea event. Yes, the isolated event that has been the sole cause of so very much of himself's anguish and self searching and doubting and decisioning for the past days, weeks, months even. And yes the dreaded event also whose end himself could only realistically though fatalistically lump into the one too staggering for comfort thought that whatever happens happens whenever and however and whyever and wherever at its end. So it was necessary for our himself to say this second "all right" this bang "all right." And so this event begins while the entire episode continues.

With himself bustlike still atop this second story vistaed promontory of our proud herself, and together they ride a swell hump to its height only to then slide, glide, slip and begin to broach to into the coming up swell valley depth that is below and opening, that is not bright cold star surface sprinkled now that the wind that rises every evening every spring has arisen again to ruffle then wrinkle its once calm pretty face. And with the greater and then greater distance from shore the wind then rose more even more still and again and again upon itself in a steady with the distance increasing progression, until now it is blowing a pure gale, a real chain link snapper as the high tiders say. And this wind progression transmits directly into a swell progression that increases steadily with the greater distance also, from just nearly swells to two to four foot swells to the six to eight foot swells that we had and dramatically to the twelve to fifteen foot swells that we now have that have stored within them for constant use a mighty work effect that is the combined resultant sum of the wind and the current and their each velocity and direction and the shove of the bulk and the shear of the mass and the jarring effect of this mighty work sum upon our himself here atop herself is a bowing and a rising and a rolling and a pitching and a yawing all at the same disorienting time simultaneously, that would suddenly greenly continuously sicken all inlanders, but did not yet and probably would not at all green sicken himself here still with both brutalized hands gripped to the big stainless steel wheel, with the pedalested captain's chair pushed hard back upon its swivel into its bulkhead recess so that himself would have plenty, plenty of get about   maneuvering space, because surely certainly he would soon need it must have it. With the only on lights still being the dim forward compass light and the above and over there stark engine room monitor picture light. While outside and to either side, the still down and the still locked horizontal abeam opposing outriggers, first one then the other and then the one again are rolling dipping and dragging into the wind ruffled wrinkled starless and moonless reflected swell hump and valley water, and slashing, gashing at this ever always moving working dark water deeply and scatteringly and tearing, and turning it into flung foam and violent spume and tossed shower sparks as each outrigger tip performs like many time magnified flat rocks that are being one time water skipped, first slung from the port side, then slung from the starboard side, then slung from the port side again, from a pitching yawing bank. With the two gushing ribbon exhausts trailing fast and gale blowing lost quickly aft into this night. With herself trembling heavily from her plunging hiding bow to her lifting ass showing a peek-a-boo stern, and rumbling bowel deep and massively and twin diesely, as again inside, himself's brutalized left hand now is loose from the big wheel and thrusts itself forward so that scarred fingers can grip himself's on and off running light switch that has remained off for so very long but which himself now clicks on for two seconds, one thousand and one, one thousand and two, then clicks off for three seconds, one thousand and one, one thousand and two, one thousand and three, then clicks on again for two seconds. And this is repeated three times precisely, as himself's opening half of the signal, as himself's half of the recognition plan, as himself's half of the I'm who I'm suppose to be and I'm definitely not who I damn well better not be signal sequence. And once this sequence is complete and there is sufficient pause, then from the much nearer now and somewhat slowed forward speed freighter comes the beginning of the counterpart' s half of the recognition plan, as the freighter's running lights are then clicked on for four seconds and clicked off for three seconds, and this signal sequence is repeated three times precisely, just as himself's sequence had been repeated three times precisely also. And so here present is the counterpart's half, the yes I'm also who I'm suppose to be and I'm also definitely not who I damn well better not be half. So for now everyone can relax secure at least for brief moments, and for now everyone can forget about frantically breaking off contact and panically running at full ahead forward speed from getting caught, trapped by a decoy, a set up, and so it is perfectly alright for us both to continue to approach, and it is perfectly alright for us both to go ahead and come together and go ahead and get on with the exchange, this transfer, and go ahead and actually begin this the goal, the purpose, the main event. And so as the two vessels then approached to nearer and nearer still, himself could begin to see some of the once again darkened freighter's details. Because himself could now see the large and spreading areas of partially scraped rust, and the large and spreading are as of partially chipped paint, with these like ugly patchwork connected hull cancers, and see the absence of new paint anywhere and this was like something sloven and intentional. And in the light from the sliver moon and the many bright stars that somewhat lighted this night, but did not reflect upon the wind furyed and foamed water, himself could also now see suddenly and startlingly, the four dim figured men who stand staring hard and fixed in a frozen line along the rail that is high above and there on the freighter's captain's bridge, where a big round faced searchlight also stands on its chest high upright mount and is bracketed for guick smooth movements in any and in all directions and is off now but is only idle and waiting to be oned in an instant a heartbeat by yet another dim figure man who is frozen in place and hard staring fixed also. And himself could see in this same sudden startling look that the four lined at the rail men each have high power automatic rifles posed up and at the trigger ready. And even though the correct signal sequences already have been communicated and these with prescribed precious timing, the four riflemen and the searchlight man still stand like deadly signal sequences already have been comm. ready menaces stalkers even looming there high above by comparison to himself ready menaces stalkers even looming there hig and herself. So himself said, "Jesus, these fuckers mean business," outloud here in this still closed wheelhouse, but this is simply a passing thought, and it is not a fear thought a panic thought, and it is simply an outloud confirmation of what he already knew to be true and knew was to be expected, and besides he the

94

trawler is who he is supposed to be and they the freighter are who they are supposed to be so there is not a problem there and besides are who they are suppose to be so there is not a and also there are plenty yes plenty of real problems yet ahead that must be met squarely and must be solved quickly indeed, yes indeed and most definitely.

The first of these real and fast approaching problems is to get herself our herself ready for the physical joining together, the actual taking possession of the goods, the responsibility transfer. And the first problem on the list within that overall large problem of getting herself ready is to get both outriggers up and locked, and as himself now began to think about the accomplishment of this he then grimly felt the full difficult and dangerous impact of Oscar's absence as mate, as coworker, as well as the inferred and the actual significant of this of being at sea absolutely alone and without a backup or any assistance of any kind, so that resultantly he himself literally would have to do the everything that had to be done, while at the same time be his own companion and be his own assurance and be his own insurance. And the first difficult and dangerous impact of this mate absence, this coworker absence, is that Oscar particularly especially like to hand control the outrigger's up and down positions there from his station at the stern work deck rather than himself having the automatic controls here in the wheelhouse. So granting this seemingly small at the time concession he had rewired the controls so that Oscar could have complete control from there. But now significantly grimly even and again, our himself would have to go aft and hand do the actual doing of the uping and the locking of the outriggers, this while leaving our herself free to swing to, to broach to and to roll to heavily and freely deeply, here among these hard bulk shoving swells, because herself's automatic pilot would be of only limited value would be of only partial success here in such heavy weather and at such close quarters with the nearer still nearer and the huge by comparison freighter. But, and but again, leaving herself free wheeling is certainly not wise and that is an understatement, nor is it intelligent even and that is an utter understatement. Because leaving herself's wheel unattended approaches and achieves total stupidity and is wild gambling in the most reckless sense, because in that crazy situation our himself and our herself' lives would be layed fully on the line and left entirely to chance, and the sea dearly loved this loves it whenever she is tempted so. And to be sure she then will go suddenly buildingly into multiple orgasms of pure delight of pure ecstasy of three big orgasms shatteringly followed by five little orgasms shakingly and in secession. And these repeated in a gushingly sloppy series for the whole all of the chance period, this while the suspense and the dread and the asshole puckering fear itself reaches deafening proportions, until finally and at last and once again at last out of our himself's control is restored over the crazy situation over the wheel over the stupid gamble. But the uping and locking of the outriggers has to be done, in fact must be done before he can get close enough along side for the transfer. And this is yet to be done, and there is only

96

himself aboard to do it, what with Oscar's absence. And as long as he is going that far to the line with the reckless gamble he may as well slide back and lock the double doored hold covering while he is at it, because that too must be done is yet to be done also for the storage of the goods from the freighter. So once again deciding to begin he takes a deep breath then sighs a quick exhale and begins, as himself makes a slow turn and brings herself slowly up past the freighter's stern, with the freighter now dead in the water in idle and patiently waiting. But the twelve to fifteen foot swells are only playtime things to the freighter there bobbing and rolling harmlessly as though being playfully teased by the sea, while at the same time these same swells are doing simple havoc with our herself as himself brings her close off the freighter's portside, the leeside, so that out of the wind somewhat and with the freighter in between as a smoothing buffer the swells' havoc would be greatly reduced though still serious and still effective and still harmful. And once in this smoother buffered lee now he pulls herself out of gear and into idle also, and then with two thin ropes he nimbly ties off the wheel from separate wheel spokes to whichever handles are convenient on opposite sides of the wheelhouse, to stop wheel spinning, to stop hard rudder turns to either side, but this will not prevent drift nor will it make necessary maneuver corrections and it is only a bandaid on a serious wound treatment. Then having already begun and being well into this newest of beginnings, himself is out of the wheelhouse and down the ladder and is bull charging aft to up and lock the outriggers and to slide and lock the hold doors, and to live for these everything on the line moments with the cold fear that only a drawn tight asshole situation can bring. But this is not a crippling fear, not is it an irrational fear, like the fear that an unfamiliar thud in the night suddenly awakened confused can bring, or like the fear that a strange city street can bring where unknown scary shadows continually shift and shuffle and move about. But rather it is a controlled flow and steadily released fear, like the fear that all professional men have who work in dangerous places and quite near to harm and to hurt and to death, like high steel men on narrow walkways who frequently dangle as they construct skyscrapers a beam at the time and a column at the time, and like dizzy speed sport car racers who delicately negotiate enclosed road tracks a bend at the time a rise at the time and the esses one at the time. Because they are professionals, and they have all been there before and many times, and they each understand fully and accept fully the risks and the work and the rewards and the penalties.

Just as himself has been upon a violent trawler stern before and many times and now is once again, and with the outriggers at last up and locked and with herself captainless still and all this time and wild swinging and top heavy badly and suddenly, now she begins rolls that are far exaggerated and far extreme and seemingly only will end with herself bottom up keel up and capsized. Then just as one gunnel is awash with seawater, herself stubbornly bravely even ceased and stops that far extreme roll somehow and someway in desperate struggle, only to begin another far exaggerated roll in the other direction, and stops this certain to capsize roll only just in time and at the absolute limit where a mere fraction of a degree more of roll and herself with himself would be capsized and dead and sea got and sea kept until she decides to give them both up, crusted and bone gaunt and barnacled and ghostly. Then with herself well into yet another sickeningly endless roll, himself finally has the hold doors slid open and themselves locked, while herself remains captainless and turned to broached to as the wash that floods in rushes over the gunnels with each far roll has the entire stern work deck under running white seawater as heavy swells of it begin to enter the hold in cascades, with himself knee deep in it and soaked through thoroughly by it, with it buffeting and tossing him about like a rag man toy doll and bashing himself against this and against that and scraping him against this and against that, until all finished for now he at last regains the ladder rails that rise in tiers and lead by levels to the wheelhouse. Where once inside with himself wide eyed excited by the furious activity and by the close at hand danger with himself sopping soaked and his clothes streaming seawater that immediately collects in spreading pools upon the deck he quickly ons the hold bilge pump toggle switch and offs the thin ropes that opposingly lash the big wheel, and then corrects for the broach to as herself has her trusted and her familiar captain once again, as slowly he again brings her along side the huge by comparison rusted and paint flaked freighter with the riflemen and the search light man still poised ready at their high above him station. But now with crewmen also lined at the rail aft at the cargo on loading and off loading deck areas, and all of these men are staring down at the small, tiny even, by comparison trawler in total disbelief and in near horror, because the trawler had just returned somehow someway alive still intact still, from the absolute brink of a vessel at sea disaster, with the disaster surely impossible to prevent once it has become so clear and present. And when himself sees fully the bewildered disbelief that is in all of their stares he says two separate and distinct words out loud with the first word being "Jesus!" because he understands completely just how truly close the call had been, and with the second word being "Oscar!" because with Oscar aboard such utter foolishness as that crazy risk had been would not have been necessary in the first place. But it is over at least for now and done at least for now, and anytime later and whenever he wants to, he can piss in his pants from the residual reoccurring fear of it, because the outriggers are up and locked and the hold doors are slid and locked and herself is properly corrected and familiarly captained now, so the goods transfer can begin actually now in fact now that this single event continues its progress. This single event itself within this overall searun itself, which already has so altered him and which will continue to effect and to affect him for all of the days of his life as only such specific events can. And which will soon also alter and effect and affect the remaining daily lives of each of the hundreds, thousand even strangers, who in the weeks and in the months to come cash purchase their unbaled, and their leaves stripped from the major stalks, and their water soaked, and their many, many times divided and redivided, and their plastic sandwich bag repackaged portions of these soon to be transferred goods, that result from this single event, with the portions then having become widely distributed merchandise that is readily openly even, available by the nickel bag and the dime bag for the schoolyard young people and by the quarter bag and the fifty cent bag for the older street people and by the pound brick and the kilo brick for the more mature and more prosperous professional people.

And then in the security of a tightly shuttered house, or in the isolation of an open park, or in the safety of a sheltered corner of a crowded crowd, each customer of whichever group can, at their leisure, spread the contents of their personal portion of the merchandise, and between hands crumple it, so that the minor stalks can be removed for toilet flushing and the seeds can be removed for either planting or for toilet flushing also, and when the three fourths that remains by weight and not by volume that is useful and is valuable has been so very carefully placed in their carrying around bag, then with a knowledgeable forefinger extended, the whichever customer can thump out a splash of the coarsely shredded and by now much traveled tobacco in a thickly scattered line upon wafer thin and new crinkly paper, then wet lick the paper edge and roll themselves a funny cigarette of absolute delight as a special present to themselves. And light it, then inhale the precious smoke deeply while also sucking sides of mouth airily, before exhaling slowly and nasally as ever so surely their cares and their woes lessen in demanding importance and commanding attention and disperse from closely nagging clusters and become not nearly so real and so insistent or so many, so that for short moments it is recess time again, kickback and relax time again, when I'll then once again take up shoulder and resume the fight, face the odds, survive the despair, cope with the uncopeable, bear the pain, deal with the tragedy, hope against hopelessness, struggle against the unchangeable, and otherwise butt heads against the all that is inevitable and is inescapable. But for now and for this while, another inhale if you please, and this time the inhale is especially deep and truly far into the lungs while again sides of mouth sucking in a quantity of air also, to dilute the marijuana smoke, but only as much as is necessary so that a sudden and an involuntary cough from its harsh strength will not happen to expel quickly and completely this narcotic cloud and thereby waste it, both from a treasured stimulant standpoint as well as from a financially expensive standpoint. So the airily deep inhale is then held and held some more and held still, there far in the lungs until the sensitive membranes there can have time to absorb as much as possible of the narcotic agent, until having held it as long as bearable the entire exhale is with a blow out and away, and is just at the point of heart pounding, racing even suffocation, but even so, some of the narcotic is still contained in the exhaled smoke and so it is lost forever preciously stimulating commodity that this is, unless by chance your date is handy and is willing to be kissed an open mouth exchange of smoke kiss, or else self centered greedily you exhale into a paper bag for temporary smoke storage until moments later when it can be retrieved. And all this as the narcotic induced wave rises and sweeps and soars you away and beyond, while a very pleasant sensual even time stagger, then time exaggeration then time warp begins, as everyone elses' life journey appears to slow down to slow motion. Or at least so you imagine while your own life journey speeds up and closes in on approaching the speed of light, or again at least so you imagine, and yourself and all and everything is enhanced and enhanced yet again upon itself until a life time of living is reduced then compressed then further compacted into but a blurred kaleidoscope flicker image of only a second's duration. This while the senses of touch and of sight and of hearing and of smell and of taste are enhanced also and enhanced yet again and also, until you can actually hear a thick slice of smoked country ham, and its voice and its sight and its touch and its smell and its taste become a once in a lifetime figment of your imagination banquet. But wisely you abstain from tasting even a mouthful of this figment feast, because even so little as a bite of this figment food once chewed and swallowed and in the stomach gets quickly into the bloodstream and once there diminishes then squelches the narcotic dream spell. And besides, actual hunger is its own enhancer also, and it enhances the other enhancers tremendously, but there is still the ham slice to hear, touch, smell, see, though not to taste, this platonically abstractly even, and to enjoy immensely and so you do enjoy it immensely while still you are being swept along on this, your self induced and self created compacted time warp flicker image. And for this brief time it is truly a wonderful journey of very pleasant sensuality that you are upon. But, ah sorrowfully, it cannot continue because all things must and do surely end, and particularly the good things, the best things, yes, especially these. As here toward this certain end, the warp becomes distortion, that becomes cycledelic, that becomes nausea, because you have traveled too far too fast while being too all alone and it is too much too soon with you so completely self contained like a jet shot bullet that is passing fiery through a slow motion background like an incandescent projectile that is passing through a slowly spiraling and a gradually closing tunnel. And like a triggered round that is traveling at fast approaching the speed of light with its appropriate pale to a darker blue all around aura, that then becomes a triggered round that is traveling at the actual speed of light itself with the aura having progressed to appropriately red all around. And it is here at such a truly blurred speed that the destructive paranoia begins, because suddenly overwhelmingly devastatingly, you become positively absolutely even, convinced that the government narcs have antenna strategically positioned on many sites through this nation, as well as this hemisphere, as well as the world, and the single purpose, mission even, for these many antenna, is to detect the super normal and the far beyond thought waves of those so few and those so rare even people who are really actually finely tuned in, and are armchair propped back, and are traveling mentally upon a strange journey of the mind, upon a journey of pure imagination and pure fantasy both finely tuned, such as yourself, yes, certainly such as yourself. And it is these many antenna that have been directionally searching continually for all such daring lone mental travelers, who incidently have been recently increasingly labeled publically as the worst of criminals, desperados even, can you believe that, that now have reduced solidified precipitated even, their vast sweeping search to only the most daring, the most alone, the most determined finely tuned mental traveler of them all. To you, yes, to you, to you yourself and to you only, and chillingly in this instant you realize also that now finally they have by accurate triangulation located you, and they have pin pointed you to within mere inches of this, your propped back precise armchair location, and very soon now they will coldly collar and impersonally bust you harshly and professionally. Because they are all around and they are everywhere and they are close and closer still now, and all this is so very real and so truly scary and now they have literally hundreds of binoculars trained hidden from trees from roof tops, from between scrubs, from through keyholes, from around corners, from even across this room of yours and also from the partially open closet door there. And aimed all at you, this their only precipiated mission target objective now, for this their vast nationwide, continentwide, hemispherewide, worldwide search as closer and closer they come stealthily pursuing, creepingly, stalking until now finally you are surrounded and you are caught in the act and you are run to the ground. But seriously I mean, really seriously, was it actually worth it for two thousand grim and armor vested agents to spend three million dollars on this so pitifully small and insignificant an effort, this effort of locating and surrounding and capturing you, you and you alone, no, of course not, because what was the true harm, I mean really. Ah, but wait, yes, and laughingly so, the joke is on them because you in the end have an out, a brilliant escape, a get away at the last minute in a hail of gunfire, through a secret passageway, to a swift horse and then over the last hill and into the sunset. Because you can always and anytime and at the last minute even, go ahead and gorge yourself on the smoked country ham that you have been this long hearing, and so you do it, make your brilliant escape, as you imagine taking up the thick juicy slice in hand and then imagine feasting upon this figment banquet feast, big bite after big bite. And just as soon as this figment food enters your stomach then it is into your bloodstream also, and in this instant the time warp vanishes, that so sensual warp, that so journeyed you through the blue and into the red euphorically, from this your traveling mentally far and wide and beyond even armchair, and with this vanishment the two thousand surrounding and closing closer government narc agents vanish, and together with them the figment ham that so coveted thick slice vanishes also. Until it is like being snatched quickly, bodily even, from the increased shrinking, collapsing even, and now reverse spiraling tunnel, until you have been suddenly returned once again to the here and to the now and to this very place where it all began, and you are again as normal as you can ever be after living and loving such a delicious and a so fantastic journey.

And it is while observing such a journey as this one that we are reminded that the human compulsion for many life journeys, for varied life journeys, for strange life journeys even, whether these are real or these are imaginary, is truly necessary and through this reminder their need is reinforced, is reconfirmed and it is this continual daily even compulsive assembly of the lesser journeys in collage that gradually manufactures our overall life journey, our complete life journey. Because it is the arrangement and it is the pattern produced by all the pieces that finally make up the whole, and it is only vital in passing, whether these lesser journeys are short or they are long, whether these lesser journeys are important or they are insignificant, whether these lesser journeys are adventures or they are drudgery, vital only that these lesser journeys happen in the first place. And it is we ourselves who finally decide the degree of the involvement, the extent of the commitment, the amount of the risks, that we are willing to assume while living these lesser journeys that produces the finished picture of the patterned assembled pieces. And even though one lesser journey may be mental while another lesser journey may be actual is also only vital in passing, because in effect in result they both can be equally damaging physically and equally jarring emotionally, according to the strength of participation of the participant. Because at the right time and in the right place and to the right person even this lesser journey of the rolling and the smoking of the joint, the reefer, the hit, of these soon now to be transferred goods, can assume the same critical impact that this hazardous searun itself has assumed.

This staggering and personally monumental searun that now has himself our himself still atop herself, and still so pitted against such heavy odds, still clearly wearing danger as such a snug garment to the extent that this searun itself has become huge in and of itself and an epic by itself because of its seriousness and because of its isolation and because of its ramifications. So therefore this searun can justifiably be divided into two separate but related and dependent events. And because the outbound run and the inbound run are such alike reflections, are really just two sides of the same coin, then reasonably they can be combined into the first single event, just as a long hike up a mountain and a long hike down a mountain can be combined into a single event. And even though mountain hikes are hazardous, ocean hikes are far more hazardous, because all and everything that happens upon the ocean includes far more hazards by definition. But even these ocean hike hazards pale in comparison to the certain perils inherent in the second event of this division of two events, to the certain perils inherent in the middle event, the sandwiched in between event, pale in comparison to the perilous time that is to be spent, to be lived, to be endured even, here at the ocean mountain summit itself. With this perilous summit time of however long a duration that it will have, being the time that is to soon begin time, the transfer between stranger vessels time, the moment of truth time, of this spectacular second event that is about to take place here and now. Here in such a still so high swelled and still so wind churned and still so current swept arena, that is this span, that is this vast concave that is Onslow Bay here still midway between Bogue Inlet and New River Inlet and still thirty five nautical miles offshore. And just as a mountain summit is lofty and panoramic and startling amid its spread mountain ranges, so too this ocean summit is lofty and panoramic and startling amid its spread mountain ranges. As slowly, so breath holding slowly, himself our David Midgett once again eases herself our Bright Dawn nearer and nearer still by mere feet at the time increments to almost alongside the rusted and the flaked paint and the absence of new paint freighter that still towers so high above herself, which somehow is a little surprising though it should not be because when among the trawler fleet of this coast herself towers above all of the other surrounding trawlers. But then this particular darkened freighter has a menace aspect somehow that herself has never and will never have and it is probably from this threatening hint that the surprise and the disconcertion results, and also it is probably something related to this improper place and at this improper time and for this improper purpose and to the sinister feel that these all have that springs the surprise and the disconcertion. But then when upon an ocean one vessel is always bigger than another vessel and sinisterism does not naturally follow or necessarily follow bigness, and however big a vessel is, there is always a vessel on a somewhere ocean that is bigger. But however big, gigantic even, the biggest vessel of all is, no vessel is really ever big enough when any somewhere ocean decides to remind all of the vessels that are upon her just how truly miniature they actually are in relation to her absolute immensity and to her potential intensity and this is especially true of this ocean this Atlantic Ocean and is very often true and is very often repeated also.

So with all of this hanging heavily about him and wearing heavily within him, himself now and once again said, "Oscar!" outloud reverberatingly here throughout this closed wheelhouse. But this "Oscar!" is a still different "Oscar!" because it is an involuntary call for assistance for help even, a sharp plea flung our while the last "Oscar!" had been merely a statement and a statement that lacked specific meaning, only a name called in this night's dimness, and a still different "Oscar!" because suddenly himself realized overwhelmingly the full impact of his situation, was finally facing squarely this huge question of how the hell could the many bales that were to be transferred possibly be received onboard and be handled and be stored correctly for weight, distribution, and then be secured in place single handedly without wobbly walking and smashed faced Oscar hard working the sterndeck as he did so cleverly and so skillfully, so loyally. How, yes indeed, how, but surely this was impossible and certainly at some later time, some future critical time, there would be a ruinous cargo shift bulkily to either side that would cause herself to list dangerously, catastrophically even, here in these still rolling and still pitching and still bowing swells. So himself said an outloud "Jesus!" that followed the outloud "Oscar!", because he just then and suddenly again realized that he had made a bad omission in forethought, a serious error in planning, a faulty miscalculation in strategy, because his first concern and the overriding concern had been to not involve Oscar in any way in this last resort and this no alternative business, just as it is natural and instinctive for him to always overprotect an innocent child from a trouble that the child cannot comprehend and from a hurt that the child should not be exposed to, because he himself could do it himself , he thought, and he himself would do it himself, he thought, because after all he had gotten himself into this bind so he would get himself out of this bind and alone.   And he really could handle it all himself, he thought, but and this was a big but, now realizing fully suddenly this one thing, this cargo handling thing, this overlooked thing, this known but forgotten about thing, that he could not possibly do himself alone. Because he simply could not be everywhere at the same time, keeping herself from sideswiping in crushing gunnel bashes the freighter while correctly cargo storing also. So what the hell was he going to do, but he did not know and then, and this again suddenly, he did know what the hell he was going to do, and into immediate action upon this quick desperate idea, he was out of the wheelhouse and running, charging even and again, toward the bow and once there he grabbed up an armful of the coiled ready bowline end and steadied himself legs spread and feet braced and readied the rope for tossing high to the freight handlers who still stood in awe and in disbelief, bewilderment even, because of the recent ocean antics of himself and herself.   And they were immobile, transfixed even, there lining the rail and looking down at him now there at the bow and now there with the bowline posed ready for tossing up to them. Because his sudden desperate idea was to lash herself first by bowline then by sternline, with used tires for gunnel fenders in between, to the freighter which would free himself considerably if not ideally, as Oscar's presence would have done, at least adequately, at least long enough for him to be pretty well at both places at the same time, and sterndeck in particular, at least until the cargo could be transferred and could be properly secured. And even though sideswiping bashes would still happen probably hopefully these would not be severe enough to cause any major structural damage to herself, because certainly she could not harm this tough hulled old freighter, but certainly this tough hulled old freighter could stove in her more fragile hull quite easily. But gradually and one by one the immobility of the freight handlers was broken and this was as if they had finally fully realized his bowline grabbing and readying intent by slow motion, until one by one, then finally all of the lined freight handlers were waving their arms above their heads at him frantically and emphatical also, waving him off from tossing up the bowline, no, no, no, and shaking their heads back and forth, no, no, no, frantically and emphatically and shouting no, no, no, frantically and emphatically also. But he could only stand at the ready there momentarily puzzled by these three different kinds of, no, no, no's, all jumbled together. But then yes, yes, well of course, of course, because in the event that a fast get away became necessary, demanded, commanded even, they did not want himself and herself lashed to their freighter, bound to their freighter, in any way to slow down, to delay, to impede their fast get away race back to the crowded shipping lanes, where once there the marshals and the customs agents would be less likely, in the confusion of many passing vessels, to board their particular freighter and arrest them for marijuana smuggling. And when he then looked higher and above forward of the freight handlers he saw that the same line of riflemen now had their rifle butts up and pressed hard to their shoulders, and that their rifles were aimed down and directly at him, fan shaped like a firing squad lined and aiming at its single victim. And then he knew and knew well indeed that if he even so much as began the bowline toss he would be instantly a many shotted dead man, because this was a most serious and a most deadly business to these harsh men, these cruel men, these greedy men. Because they have done this many times before. Because they have been successful at least so far because they take absolutely no unnecessary chances. Because they minimize absolutely all risks completely and entirely to their advantage. But so what the hell was he going to do, because a bad option is better than no option at all, because at least it is some kind of an option, some kind of action, and he had quickly just about run out of options of any kind what-so-ever since there were only several to begin with. But he still did not know what he was going to do, so it was drop the bowline armful in place and charge back into the wheelhouse again. And once there he spun the big wheel to hard port and slammed the gears into forward and shoved the throttle to full and sharply pulled away from lying so very dangerously close to along side the freighter, to give himself time to think, to give himself time to plan a plan, any plan, good plan, or bad plan, but at least some plan, because the freighter captain was not going to wait out here for him forever wallowing in idle out here for many more minutes. Because the freighter captain wanted this transfer begun and done and ended, and all these accomplished soon too, because the freighter captain wanted to be once again upon his innocent looking high seas way so as to not attract attention and therefore suspicion from any happen chance passersby. Because it certainly was not the freighter captain's fault if our David had not used sound judgement, sound forethought, had overlooked Oscar's critical need at a critical time, had planned well but had not planned thoroughly. So with the only option still available to him, David stepped out of the wheelhouse and stood for a moment by the rail there, and then gave the freighter handlers a slow sweeping from low to high and wide one armed come on wave signal, then he slowly again pointed to the sterndeck of herself, in saying bring it on and put in back there fellows. And with this signal, the freight handlers right away went to the winch and swing boom and they began to hoist the cargo net that already was bulging with marijuana bales, and by the time they had the heavily loaded net extended over midship and were lowering it, himself had herself once again very dangerously close alongside the freighter, and when he heard the bouncing thud of the bulging cargo net upon the sterndeck, he was again charging outside the wheelhouse and was again into the sea wind and the sea spray, and was again so close to the freighter that he could see its barnacles as individual barnacles, each small and round and raised with a hole in the center, and they were like dirty brown crystalline candy lifesavers, and he could see its hull plates and their joint seams and the fastening rivet heads that held the plates in place rigidly. And he could see the furry green algae slime that so thickly covered its bottom that the red lead bottom paint could be seen only as a dirty background pale pink. But all this was seen in fast passing, in almost registering, in almost remembered, because he was broadly taking the steps down and aft two at a time recklessly, wildly even, in a mad dash to get to the loaded cargo net that bounced then raised itself danglingly twistingly thudingly about the hold hatch opening. And now at the net and breathless and very excited, he saw for the first time in his young thirty some years the objects, here, that were the subject of so many recent clandestine meetings and so much secret whispering with vague unsmiling men, urgent men who came to talk with him, but always around corners and always among shadow, these objects that then themselves became the subject of so much lower lip chewing anguish and so many sleeplessly tossing about in decisioning nights. These objects, this subject, there that are compacted and bound burlap wrapped bales that have Columbia stenciled in black block letters on each bale, with each bale being approximately two feet square at the ends and three feet long. These bales that now are his only alternative, his last resort, his out, and the saver of our Bright Dawn herself from bank foreclosure. These bales that each weigh approximately sixty pounds, these bales that each have a street value of approximately thirteen thousand dollars, these same bales that are here now finally and have begun to be transferred now and again finally. And there are approximately fifty of them there in the first load, and bouncing there about the hold hatch opening, in the cargo net that has a tie rope at its gathered bottom, just as a trawl net has a tie rope at its gathered bottom which is called a tailbag, a tie rope so that the trawled for catch can be quickly dumped into a culling box for sorting the catch with only a hard jerk of the tie rope, this cargo net tie rope here that now he scrambles for amid the thudding and the twisting.

This tie rope that now he has hold of, and as the cargo net rises again with the swell trough fall of herself, here so very dangerously close alongside the freighter, and when the cargo net is almost directly above, as it is ever going to freely swinging going to get, he hard jerk releases the rope's simple tie knot. And when he does this then three thousand pounds of burlaped stenciled bales, a ton and a half of compacted loose bales, cascade and crash into the hold hatch opening and tumble about the hold hatch opening also, and thud individually end over end and scatter about the repeatedly ocean washed sterndeck. But he has already turned his back on all this cascading noisy confusion and momentarily he has dismissed it, because once again he is into a mad dash for the stairs and is on his wild way to the wheelhouse, where there he slams herself into gear and revs herself shutteringly from idle and pulls herself again sharply away from here, away from the freighter's somewhat more protected leeside but not much more protected leeside, not really, and out and away to where the twelve to fifteen foot swells are truly doing a pitching and a yawling dance of frenzy now. And out and away to where the wind is blowing a pure onshore direction gale now, and is building still as it has been building all along, as it heads shoreward, and has built enough already to keep the next coastal high tide floodingly backed up all along the tideland marshes and the barrier islands, and backed up into all the bays and the sounds, and backed up into all the tributaries and the creeks and the streams until even the heartiest or more correctly the hungriest of clammers even with long tongs will not have a decent honest workday the next day, poor unlucky bastards that all scrounging clammers are anyway, because if it is not a flood tide then it is always something. And with herself now in slow ahead and on automatic pilot, for whatever small good that will do, himself is again outside the wheelhouse and again aft at the hold hatch where there he begins to grab and to basketball toss the tumbled scattered remaining bales into the opening and soon no more bales remain upon the sterndeck. And then and just as quickly he is back inside the wheelhouse and then comes off automatic pilot and revs and comes about in preparation for the second of what eventually will be a total of six coming alongside the freighter onloading maneuvers, before finally he has on board three hundred bales with these three hundred bales having a combined street value of three point nine million dollars with his cut of this to be a quarter of a million dollars. Yes, a quarter of a million dollars, and that payable upon his onshore delivery, and this just for the simple hauling of the bales from here to there. Imagine that, two hundred and fifty thousand dollars worth of bank foreclosure stopper, worth of money stick with which to beat back the credit wolves. Because as always and forever, cash talks and bullshit walks. Because in this country, how you get money and where you get money is still not important. Because having money is all that is important. Because the portion of the how and the where that cannot be forgiven can be purchased, can be silenced. Because, sadly, he has recently realized that greed is still as American as is flag and mother and apple pie American.

And when he now looked up to the freighter deck he saw that the handlers had the tie rope gathered bottom tied again and that the cargo net had been loaded with another fifty bales, so it was to alongside the freighterthat he brought herself. And during his approach he again looked further up and he saw that the same line of riflemen had neither moved or even shifted stances, and that they were still there with their rifles aimed firing squad like at him wherever he was aboard herself and whatever herself's leeside position, so he said another out loud "Jesus". But this "Jesus" was only another acknowledgment of this still scary situation, this still tense situation, and another "Jesus" that lacked enthusiasm, emphasis even, Because amid true all around close danger mere tenseness and mere scariness are comparatively lesser emotions that quickly become familiar emotions. But then he heard the next loaded cargo net thud upon the sterndeck, so he was immediately outside the wheelhouse and wild running.

And now it is awhile later, and when he has just pulled herself away from alongside for the fourth time, that he can feel a definite and an increasing portside list to herself that obviously is resulting from the already loaded bales being too much distributed to that side. And it is exactly this sort of screw up that Oscar would have prevented if he were aboard and hard working as usual and avoiding even small screw ups before they snowball and become real problems. But Oscar is not on board, no, himself rudely saw to that so here you have more spilt milk and as always there is no need to cry over spilt milk, because what is done is done, and there you have it so to hell with it. But a screw up while at sea cannot be dismissed, because it does not go away as if by magic, and you cannot ignore it, because it always returns to haunt you and always at the worst possible time too. So what remains is to squarely face the screw up, to correct it, or to nullify it at least, and you must try to do either at least try, and if after really trying you fail to do either then stoically you learn to live with the screw up and the ramifications, however slight or however severe that the resulting problem brings with it. So and accordingly, on the next on loading pass our himself tries to throw the scattered loose bales so that they would land far to the starboard side in the hold, to hopefully begin to even the distribution. But throwing this many sixty pound bales, one after the other, after the other, instead of lightly tossing them basketball like, and throwing them while bending far over and leaning far over also, is simply too physically exhausting, and himself has already reached near exhaustion anyway, because of the wild running, because of all the frantic activity of maneuvering herself, because of all the mental strain and the mental drain of having to be both places, wheelhouse and sterndeck, at about the same time. So stoically he stops trying to redistribute the weight, having decided to live with the increasing portside list and the ramifications which it will surely bring with it as a later on real problem. Because all of this has suddenly become too much, too concentrated, too overwhelming, because now he is getting confused, because now he is getting panicky, these from the too many critical demands begin placed upon himself alone and in so short a time. But also because a more pressing problem, a here now problem, is closer at hand and is one that he must contend with calmly and here and now. So somehow he must dispel his confusion, somehow he must surpress his panic, because in addition, as if anything else were needed on top of everything else, these pure gale force winds that have already arisen upon themselves several times and have caused these swells to therefore arise upon themselves several times also, have once again arisen upon themselves and have produced in resulting direct ratio fifteen to seventeen foot swells within what has truly become a terrible blow now. With these long, long, slow high swells having become a moaning series, an endless series, of soaring heaves and sickening troughs and disorienting slides up to a heave and down to a trough endlessly. With five seconds for a heave to pass, and five seconds for a down slide to pass, and five second for a trough to pass, and five seconds for an up slide to pass and these passing and passing long and slow and moaning with each separate series repeating itself exactly every twenty seconds and again and again and again, until the fact of just begin out here in a trawler of no matter how the hell big has gone way, way beyond folly and has reached utter stupidity, even if Oscar were aboard, and is absolute madness and is absolute suicide but is particularly so, especially so even, by being out here alone, all alone. But alone he has been and alone he is and alone he will be until whatever happens finally happens at whatever end there will be to this searun.

And now as himself is coming about to come alongside the freighter for the fifth time, for the next to the last time, herself, our herself, does an unexpectedly deep bow, a surprisingly even deep bow, and then continues this deep bow by nosing heavily into an upslide toward a heave, and straight into the bulk of this thick swell, as though herself suddenly has become a cut loose anchor that is plunging, racing even, toward the far below sea floor. And with the bad portside list, our herself rolls drunkenly portside also together with the nosing, the plunging, the falling far down, and all around and everywhere there is now only the darkness of this thick seawater, which is much darker than this merely dim night. And with the swamping, this smothering, himself, our himself, instantly realizes, then instantly knows for certain, that this time herself would never, could never right herself, would never, could never recover herself, no, not this time. So this is it, so this is how it ends, so unexpectedly, so surprisingly, so suddenly, with a nosing in that becomes a plunge, a fall, and a roll, that becomes a keel up, a belly up, so now it is to be a hearty hello to you long crusted old dad, there below in your cold deep seawater grave, and a hearty hello also to all of you other crusted bluewatermen, to all of you who have come to be so very long lost at sea after having sought, embraced, cherished even, harm, real sea harm, and too often, and then finally once too often. So our himself said yet another "Jesus!", but he damned well meant this "Jesus!", because it would be his last "Jesus!", and it echoed in the seawater covered, now seawater smothered wheelhouse as a laughing happy yell, because of this one hell of a wild, delirious even, last ride to the far bottom. Because once having accepted dying and actual death as inevitable as inescapable, then the threshold beyond which there is no personal fear has been reached and crossed. But with this happy "Jesus!" still echoing joyfully, then the thick seawater began to thin and began to part and to pass and to be shedded there from the all around forward glass, because somehow, someway, herself had bravely buoyed herself enough, just enough, to bow up herself, and to break through the heave and to come out with her bow proudly extended and seawater parting protruding like a maidenhead ram from the downslide, and then for her rescued bow to fall with a loud plop of a flung everywhere splash into a slow trough.

So this particular real sea crisis was over and just as quickly as it had begun, because there still close by was the still sluggishly lumbering flaked painted freighter.   And having been just this quickly snatched back from dying and from death itself, our himself involuntarily and unaware of it recrossed that special threshold and returned to here where personal fear is a perfectly normal reaction to danger.   And he then immediately switched on herself's main bilge pump as well as herself's backup emergency bilge pump, because having come under that heavy heave with the hold hatch open like an inviting yawn herself for sure will have taken on a ton of seawater.   And with this done and as though nothing miraculous had just happened, he then continued to come alongside the freighter for the fifth time, for the next to the last time.   But while he was waiting to hear the announcing thud of another loaded cargo net upon the sterndeck, herself did yet another hard portside roll because of the influence of her bad portside list, and this was followed by an exaggerated and compensating starboardside roll. But while this was going on the freighter was also into a lumbering roll of its own and to its portside, and with these two vessels now way too close alongside each other, it was natural that they would collide, this small by comparison trawler and this huge by comparison freighter, and with a bash that was an end of the world bash, a hail and farewell bash, so that herself's tall tapered outriggers set into whiplashing themselves with a pure din of noise of cables slapping steel and cables slapping other cables.   And on herself's next starboardside roll that side outrigger snapped its up and lock cable as though it were a string, and with this, that side outrigger hit the freighter with a solid blow, a crushing blow, that then stoved in the rail and the cabin bulkhead and the several portholes that were there on that particular upper deck. And with this the firing squad line of poised ready riflemen picked up and suddenly hauled ass for cover, orders or no orders, every man for himself and may the devil take the hindmost. And later our himself would have a real good chuckle when his mind reran the mental picture of their fast scampering, because even rigid deadly serious men, men who would blow you away, literally at any false move, will pick up and run like a bat out of hell whenever a loosed outrigger suddenly seeks to give then a popping head bop. But being more aft and below and therefore safely out of the runaway outrigger's stoving in range, the freight handlers had stayed their ground, so when himself heard the cargo net again thud upon the sterndeck he was out of the wheelhouse and charging for it. But just as he had hold of the tie rope and had a steadying grip on the cargo net itself, herself fell with a trough while the freighter raised with a heave, and then in only a second everything became all movement and in all four directions at the same time because in that instant there he was aloft and ten feet above herself's sterndeck with one hand gripping the cargo net and the other hand holding the tie rope, with himself just midair dangling there like a key wound dollman that had been set into jiggling four way motion. So he hollered "oh shit!!" as loud as he could, which was way beyond a yell and approaching a scream even, to anyone and to everyone and to no one especially. But no sooner had he hollered this, then in the next second there he was crashingly sprawled out upon the sterndeck, dollman all fall down like, when next the freighter fell and herself raised. But wait!, because the cargo net was close behind also, and closing fast too, with its enclosed ton and a half of loaded bales and coming down hard to crush him. So in that instant he jerked the tie rope and released his net steadying grip and began a sideways roll of his very own, but then in a blur, you could not see him

for all the then loosed bales that had commenced to tumble and to jumble and to scatter all about. But break out from under them and among them and atop them he did, like a trapped man possessed and breaking out come hell or high water, because our himself could pick up and haul ass with the best of them and the gone for cover riflemen included.

And then once again he was off and wild running for the wheelhouse. But when he pulled herself away from alongside the freighter this time, the loosed starboardside outrigger made a chilling goose bump rending screech as it cut a steel on steel horrible white scar along and down the side of the freighter like a knife wound. But when the outrigger hit the water it dug in like a broken arm that flops, and with the already bad list to port and the now dug in outrigger to starboard, herself wallowed heavily in these high long constant swells until it was very difficult for himself to gain enough steerage to maneuver to outside this too close by danger of the freighter. But finally having wallowed on out there, himself put herself on slow ahead, as well as on automatic pilot, and then he headed for the big handyman toolbox that is just aft of the wheelhouse and there below where the sterndeck begins. And with a sledge hammer from it, he set about to pounding out the pivotal holding pins for both outriggers that are there where they join at their common base, and once both of these pins were out and gone so that the outriggers were base freed, then he unlocked and loosed the portside outrigger at the winch until finally it also fell and flopped like a broken arm and dug in deeply on that side. And then with a pair of large bolt cutters, he set about to systematically cutting all the many cables and many lines that were still connected and flailing about and lashing about like strummed wires, until first the portside, then the starboardside outrigger had been cut free entirely, to slide overboard and to sink quickly like the merely useless dead weights that they now were, down and down and heading straight for the desert sea floor that is one hundred feet below to become rusted and barnacled small oasis for small fishes. And so it was goodbye to herself's thirty thousand dollars worth of precious trawling gear rigging. But there simply was not the time to dwell on how naked and how raped herself now looked with this so distinctively hers alone trawling gear rigging all gone, because he had already set about to gathering the scattered bales that were still sterndeck topside after that last comic and nearly disastrous unloading. And he was basketball tossing them one by one into the hold hatch opening wherever the hell they landed inside, because right now proper distribution was last on his long list of many worries. But then when himself brought herself about to come alongside the freighter for the sixth time, for the very last time, thankfully and hurrah this cargo transfer finally, yes finally, reaching its conclusion, finally reaching its seemingly endless end, everyone, every damn body, all of the freighter's crew from the stranger captain and his mates down to the freight handlers, searchlight man and the riflemen included, every damn body and the engine room gang also, were at the rails fore and aft along the several decks there rising so high above himself and herself, here in this dim light night, here among these constantly heaving, constantly falling swells, here in this blowing a pure gale wind. And everyone was waving them off from coming alongside and in harsh and in emphatic and in no shit man seriously, arm waves of enough is damn well enough, and no more of this stupidity that borders on and reaches sheer madness even, and enough particularly so for you far smaller by comparison trawler. Because this freighter can be scarred by you but you cannot damage us not truly, not utterly, but we far larger by comparison can destroy you simply and easily and completely. Because just look at the destruction that already has happened to yourself, with your precious outriggers gone and lost, with your precious cables and lines cut and fouled and in tatters, with your starboardside clearly showing the mean scrapes of our recent bash collision in glaring raw streaks of this freighter's flaked paint and this freighter's dead red lead bottom paint like nearly mortal slices down and along your far more tender by comparison hull, with yourself already listing so badly to port that you are taking heavy swell after heavy swell until increasingly now yourself is awash from stem to stern in running sluices of rushing

127

seawater like a critically crippled vessel that is almost swamped and is about to founder. So enough of this silliness man, good god enough of this foolishness. But without a second thought, without even an instant of hesitation, our himself over ruled these wave offs, shrugged off these wave offs, ignored these wave offs, and instead steps tall outside the wheelhouse like the true bluewaterman that he is. Like a bluewaterman who has often seen the ocean at her worst, who has closely lived with the ocean at her cruelest, who has long known the folly that men in vessels can practice while upon her. Until and from these experiences, her horrors finally become only a matter of degrees for him. Until and from these experiences, her challenges finally become only a matter of endurance for him. A true bluewaterman who has hard and well learned that what she presents as impossible for regular men, he can almost always reverse into the possible because tenacity is the absolute way of things for men who earn their daily living from her. Because it is only rarely that she gives up her food treasures gently or generously. Because each of their working days are merely just another day of hardship, of frustration, of pain, of futility, of despair, of determination, of insistence, of perseverance, of patience. And it is as such a man as this that our himself now stands bluewater rugged outside the wheelhouse, but inactive, thoughtful even, for only this quick moment, and then, and this deliberately, he give them all and everyone fore and aft and upon all decks, the up stuffing screw you finger defiantly and with finality.

Because this sixth and this last coming alongside is possible and it is not impossible, not yet, and it must be tried, at least tried, because everything that is begun upon the ocean must be completed upon the ocean. Because as soon as a man backs away from her in doubt in fear even briefly, even fleetingly, then he may as well tie his boat to any dock and then walk far inland to sit forever after in a rocking chair on a somewhere porch never to venture upon her again, or to see her again, or even to mention her ever again. Because she has won and she is the victor and she will always know that about this man, and he has lost and he is the vanquished and he will always know that about the ocean. And this will be a permanent defeat for him to always carry cry hurting inside like an endless cold dread, because this is the absolute way of things also.

And with our himself's brutalized hands now cupped around his no longer young mouth, he hoarsely coarsely yells into this still blowing a pure gale wind, to all of them there above lining the rails, "hoist swing and lower that last load you sorry sacks of shit, because I'm David Midgett of the trawler Bright Dawn, and the best goddamn sea captain that you'll ever see, and that's a fucking fact Jack," from boasting self elation, from approaching sure triumph. And then, and just as he had done at the first coming alongside, he gave them that slow sweeping from low to high and wide one arm come on wave signal, that once again ended with his pointing steadily toward our herself's sterndeck, in saying come on boys come on now bring it on and put it there. Because with the grinding away chaos, and with the grinding away jeopardy, and with the grinding away weariness, this entire long transfer had now become like a dream to him and dreamlike it now had all the aspects, had all the reality of a projected flicker film series, of an impersonal distant wall flashing sequence, that had only to last reel itself off through to its final episode footage scene. Because try he most assuredly would and endure he most assuredly would and these diligently, stubbornly even, and this is as much for certain as anything is ever for certain. Because even the degrees of danger had ceased to exist for him, until they no longer mattered or were they of concern. Because though the ocean could easily destroy him, she never and no not ever would defeat him. Because he simply would not, could not allow that. Because this was his.own private absolute way of things.

And so as these two vessels were now this sixth time dramatically alongside, with this last load already hoisted and already swung and now being lowered, but just before it could sterndeck thud even the first time, he had the tie rope snatched and was already halfway back to the wheelhouse, this as the burlaped bales bump landed helter skelter jumbled wherever they would. But when at the wheelhouse itself, our himself again paused to quickly find the freighter captain among the top deck rail crowd, there high above, and to hurriedly give him that special sea captain to sea captain rigid flat hand to forehead fellowship salute, which the freighter captain received warmy, then returned smartly. But during his follow through, the freighter captain also and together, smiled in pride, shook his head in disbelief, and tipped his cap, these for the well done job, though to be sure you are a crazy as hell trawler captain you are. Which our himself received on the run casually and in passing and in the split moment just before he was back inside the wheelhouse. Back as only another shadow amid the all around dimness, back before the big stainless steel wheel, there once again wheeling sharply our herself away from alongside for this final time. And thereby inbound, yes inbound our two now were, and at last and actually inbound. Because the outbound searun had long been concluded, and here just now the transfer itself had been so recently so freshly so newly brought to its own separate conclusion, therefore the tough mountain peak had been scaled, therefore the desperate stay at the summit was ended, therefore the only part of the trilogy that remained was the figurative sliding downhill searun descent inbound. And this just had the very instant of its beginning, so our himself looked at his watch and he saw that only one grueling hour had passed during the transfer part, instead of the ten hours that in his exhaustion it seemed like. So he said an almost whispered "Jesus" to himself for the irony, for the time distortion of that, then he turned and he looked astern and he saw that the once again lighted freighter already was making fast faster for the sheltered open innocence of the regular shipping lanes, that are way over yonder and are there at this night's near far horizon. But then in self preservation, in self survival even, he suddenly shook himself an inward physical outward shake to force the return of his already shabby worn thin attention to this that was here, to this that was now, and especially to all things that pertained to that even remotely were related to the care and to the protection of our himself himself and to our herself herself. An inward physical outward shake, to force the return of his already shaky ground away concentration, to redefine it, to reduce it, to narrow it, to focus it even, on that which that was immediate, on that which that would be forthcoming. To have both attention and concentration available and functional and serviceable, just as all useful valuable tools should be frequently maintained and readily accessible where they properly belong. Because being this far offshore, being so stressed and so strained, being this completely alone, he simply could not relax nor could he be idle, at least not for too long, at least not yet, at least not for too long, at least not yet, at least not quite yet, at least not for awhile yet.

Because certainly there would be plenty of time for relaxed and for idle soon and in awhile, and right after this, so again he switched on the automatic pilot for whatever small good that it would do here in this still hard blow, and in these still strong currents, and with these still heavy swells. Then, in a too action again, and a too work again rush he was out of the wheelhouse running, then aft and sterndeck tossing the jumbled about last load bales into the still open hold. But even though his mind was still sound and his mind was still willing, his too overworked in too brief a time span body was up to only half effort attempts to get these bales far to the starboardside inside the hold, for better weight distribution, so he did the best and did the most that he could do, then left it at that, because that was all he could do. But when the last bale at last had been tossed, the hold hatch opening covers were not anywhere to be found so they could not be, replaced, they apparently having been sea taken sluiced away overboard and were now lost, gone, down sunk and sea got also, just as so much upon the sea becomes sea got. So our himself just shrugged an its done and cannot be helped now shrug. Because indeed he had tried, because indeed he had endured, because indeed he was not defeated. Because the hatch covers were nickel and dime stuff, and in much too busy times the nickel and dime stuff simply cannot be sweated. Because all that remained now was the inbound piloting, and that would be just another searun. Because that would be just a downhill descent of a slightly wounded voyager who does the descent just a little cautiously, just a little tentatively. So he looked up at the startling to look at, jarring to look at even, vacant space where the two massive the two towering outriggers had been and should be, but were not, and all that remained that actually emphasized their stark absence were the dangle swinging cut cable ends and the whip snapping cut line ends that hung robbed loosed there from the still standing iron pipe latticework bracing, like the pathetic shredded remains that they were.

Then he looked higher and much farther, and he saw that the hardly even a sliver moon now had waned itself, and had cooled itself, and had lowered itself, and these considerably, and these in only the past hour, here in this bright brighter star now night sky. Then he looked lower and much closer again, and out where he saw that the still long slow sea heaves that hulkingly trailed each other one after the other after the other, had driven white scud running before them in thrown mists here in this still gale gusty wind. Then he looked quite close, and down at the harsh hands that he held palms up before himself, and he saw that they were grey pinched water puckered, and that they showed new cuts and new scrapes and new gouges, among the trying to heal and taking forever to heal cuts and scrapes and gouges, and among the finally scarred over and raised welted old cuts and old scrapes and old gouges. So he said another almost whispered "Jesus" for how gnarlly pitiful his hands looked, for how brutally painful his hands felt. But torn sore claws for hands were also the absolute way of things out here daily, weekly, monthly, yearly upon her. Then he looked up and forward to the captainless lonely the captainless empty wheelhouse, and with a sudden good surge of renewal, of cheerfulness even, he said a strong outloud "All right!" that said, 'it wasn't done pretty, but it's done now.'

CHAPTER FIVE

He had never been this dazed. He had never been this exhausted. He had never been this hungry. So he tied off the wheel then went into the galley that was just aft of the wheelhouse. Among the leftovers inside the compact refrigerator was a quart size container almost to the top with a shrimp salad of cut pink shrimp and shredded lettuce and cut up tomatoes and diced onion and salt and pepper and mayonnaise. With this he went to the sink and with a fork from the drain rack, he wolfed it down. Then he put the emptied container in the sink and ran it full of water from the spigot and tossed the fork into that to soak. Then he got the covered plate of fried flounder fillets that was among the left-overs also and put that on the counter. Then he got two beers from the refrigerator. One he put on the counter beside the fillets. The other he flip top opened then quickly drank half of it. The suddenly released carbonation started backing up on him in rising growing bubbles, so for a moment he just stood there belching air, and feeling how herself was doing with the portside list still bad but not terrible. He had his left leg straight and his right leg unlocked at the knee and that was sufficient compensation. If the list was terrible he would have had his left leg straight and his right leg bent at the knee plus be leaning against the list also. So the list was manageable for the inbound run without drastic corrective action.

And her speed was about right. If it were too slow the trailing winds would cause the trailing swells to break over her stern, and that would spell disaster. If it were too fast herself would plow into the swell ahead, and that too would spell disaster. So herself had sufficient speed for good inbound progress without either shoving ahead or being overrun astern. But it would not be a gentle inbound run not with this same hard heaving and this same hard falling and this same hard rolling. But it would be a safe inbound run and a technically correct inbound run. And the hunger had eased considerably and it no longer was painful. And with this, the daze that had so grogged his thoughts for awhile thinned then cleared. So he got mayonnaise from the refrigerator and bread from the drybox and a knife also from the rack, and with a slice spread thick he layered on two hand size fillets and covered that with a slice. Then he finished the first beer and took the second beer and the flounder sandwich forward with him to the wheelhouse. He swung out the pivot arm captain's chair from its bulkhead recess and sat in it before the wheel and wolfed at the thick sandwich in between pulls at the second beer. Then he slipped the wheel ties and resumed his captaincy and with the rest break and with the food he now felt strong again.

"'Okay!" He said with confidence with this fresh start. Then he began making plans out loud. "So we'll just put in at New River Inlet instead of Bogue Inlet. No big deal that. And that would be the sensible thing. Her steerage to starboard is spongy, and overpowering that would be a needless struggle. She wants to slide off to port with the list anyway, so grudgingly let her. And according to reckoning we'll make New River without lost time. Then up the Inland Waterway to Queens Creek. Once inside, the list won't matter that much. I'll just have to hold the wheel a bit against it. Nickel and dime stuff, nickel and dime stuff. Yeah, but remember that it's a longer leg from New River Inlet there, than from Bogue Inlet there. And that'll put us at Fulcher's Landing about thirty minutes later. Okay. Well. Okay well, that's still the best way to do it. That's still the sensible thing. Yield to the list inbound to avoid a needless struggle. Then lose time on the last leg as the price. Give and take. Good old fashioned compromise, and us trawler captains get good at that. Trade offs are a way of life when it comes to boats and the sea. Yeah, but remember that it's damn near deserted all the way from New River Inlet to Queens Creek. So there would be almost no chance of our being spotted coming that way. But once inside Bogue Inlet there would be all the waterfront lights at Swansboro for us to slip past. Then all the houses that are almost one beside the other there fronting the waterway all the way to Queens Creek. And there'll certainly be skiff fishermen out shrimping or floundering or gillnetting, in and out of all the bays around there. And the Wildlife man could even be out with his night scope trying to catch idiot people clamming in closed areas. You never know where that tricky son of a bitch is going to be or when. Yeah, we're bound to be spotted coming that way. Herself's silhouette is well known. And with the gone outriggers and the list and the sitting low as hell in the water with the load, we stick out like a sore thumb. People get mighty curious mighty fast. Then they begin to wonder out loud. People talk. Yes hell, people do talk. And it would be just plain stupid to get thrown out while crossing homeplate. So New River Inlet then up is the best way to do it. The only sensible thing. Hell, it would be the smart way even without the list. The only way really. But you hadn't thought of things like this till now, had you? Well you damn well better start thinking of things like this. Because this is hardball with big boys not marbles with small kids. And till you get this stuff off loaded, your ass is the grass and everyone else has the lawnmowers. But that's what you're getting the megabucks for. The hauling, yes, but for the risk really. Megabucks for a megarisk. But the wall to wall narcs around here don't screw around anymore than the freighter guys screwed around or the Miami guy screws around. And now you have the ball and are coming down field fast. But it's you against everyone else. Because there's only you on your team. So there's no one to run interference. No back up. No substitute. No coach. No spotter. So you damn well better do hard thinking till this is over. Because even though you're playing at home, you're playing in their ballpark. And you're playing their game. And they're writing the rulebook as they go.

"But word is that only one in ten get caught. And that's not bad odds. But that's just the word. And who knows for sure. Because the odds could be one in twenty, or the odds could be one in three. Who knows for sure. But I hope the odds ain't one in three. Because that's not good odds. At least for this. But they say

138

it's quick easy money. But they say a lot. And who the hell are they anyway? And what do they know? Because they ain't doing it. You're doing it. And so far it ain't been all that easy. Fairly quick, yes. But easy, no. Because the transfer was a real ball buster. That's a for sure. But those guys sure hauled ass when herself's loosed outrigger started chasing them. That was funny. The expressions on their faces. But none of this is funny. No, not really. It's scary as hell is what it is. Yes, it's scary as hell alright. Because here you are twenty miles out on a shaky limb, and who knows who may be busy somewhere sawing it off. And its that, what you don't know, that can hurt you. It probably won't kill you, not now, that part's over, but it can sure hurt the hell out of you. And in several ways. But one in ten ain't bad odds. No, not if they're the real odds. Yeah, unless you just happen to be the one in one in ten. Then not bad odds don't mean shit. Because you're got. And herself is seized to be sold at public action. And you're tossed in jail until Christ comes wearing tennis shoes. So you're a real trusting soul, you are. Because that Miami guy could be giving over one in ten just to keep the narcs happy. Giving them something to take to their bosses. Something to splash around in the news. Look ma no hands sort of thing. And there's pure armies of them. Because there's the Coast Guard and Customs and the Marshals and local cops and the Sheriff and the FBI and the SBI and the State Alcohol Firearm Tobacco and Tax guy. And who knows how many others all stumbling over each other. And they're jealous of each other. And each is trying to out justify the other.

And each is busy protecting themselves from the other. Their waste and double effort is beyond comic and into tragic. They're like ten ant armies scurrying to build castles in the same sandpile. But if they ever do get it together, really get it together, then heads up. Because then a seagull couldn't fart around here without their knowing it, and pouncing on him like a trawl door had been dropped on him. Maybe they did get it together. Really got it together. Just for tonight. And just for you. Surprise! That ain't funny. No, that ain't funny. It's scary. And that asshole Bobby Willis was the go between on this. But he'd have his own mom tricking if there were any takers. Then give her over for the reward if there were one. Yeah, you're a real trusting soul alright. And an assuming soul too. You're trusting that no one has given you over. And assuming that the narcs are still stumbling around among themselves. Well, lots of luck. Yeah, lots of luck, fella.

"Because suddenly you don't like any of this. Not any of this. Because there's no way you'll get away entirely clean. Because there's far too many unknowns. Because there's too much you didn't think about before, that you've only just begun to think about. Because there really wasn't time to think about all that. Because you really didn't know to think about all that. Because stopping the foreclosure was everything. And the only thing. Somehow. Someway. Anyway. Just stop it. Stop that damn foreclosure! Like the desperation to awake from a bad dream, so a fast end can be put to its nightmare. Someway. Anyway. Just stop it. Quick stop it. End It! But that was yesterday. And today's today. And you can't change the past. So it Is simply more spilt milk. And no need crying over it. And now's now. And here you are. And what's coming is what's coming. And even if the off loading goes well, you'll have to pump half the Atlantic through the hold to flush out all the residue. Because getting caught with only residue next week or next month is the same as getting caught with the whole cargo tonight. And you'll look mighty suspicious laying off somewhere just flushing the hold for three hours, like idly standing off somewhere just twiddling your thumbs. Yeah, mighty suspicious indeed. And folks around here are given to suspicious anyway, are given to curiosity anyway. Are given to wondering, and to wondering out loud. So flushing the hold is another something that you haven't thought about. That now you're thinking about. That just adds another thing to the everything else to suddenly not like about any of this. But it's too late now. Way too late now. Useless closing the barn door now. Because the horse is already out and away and heading for the finish line now. But what are you doing here in the first place? And why did you get into this in the first place? I just don't know. How would I know that? Maybe it was fate. Maybe it was circumstance. Maybe it was stupidity. Maybe it was ignorance. Maybe it was all these. Maybe it was a combination of these. Maybe it was none of these. And just the way it goes. The way the ball bounces. The way the cookie crumbles. The way the ink blots. The way the paper tears. Hell, I don't know! How would I know? I really just don't know. But there will be a time later when I'll know. For sure, for sure. Yeah, I've a strong feeling that later I'll definitely come to know a whole lot, and come to know it the hard way. But right now, this very moment, I really just don't know. So why do people blow their minds away smoking this crap in the first place? I don't know that. How would I know that?

I just don't know that either. But everyone's doing it. Yeah, they certainly are. That's another for sure. In big demand, this. In really big demand, this. So why do you drink? It's the same escape. Yeah, but drinking's legal. Big difference, that. All the difference, that. But if this were legalized and farmers here grew it and the cigarette makers manufactured it, half the smokers would quit smoking it. And the price would drop to a fourth. And the bad quality misery would be stopped. Because mostly I think it's the thrill of sneaking around breaking the law. Yeah, and it's a lot of don't dare tell me what I can and I can't do with my life. Because y'all already do way too much of that, and enough's enough. So it's playing hookey from school. It's swiping a whistle from a dime store. It's slipping into the movies. But it can be a sick habit also, to the weak, to the hooked. Just as drinking can be to those also. Because then the habit must be fed daily and in quantity, while the habit worsen and deepen still more. But at least booze is reasonably priced. And there's treatment for that and hardly ever jail for that. But the price of this can become ridiculous. Especially when it's become indispensable. And there's jail for this, and hardly ever treatment for this. Yeah, big difference. All the difference. But it doesn't really have anything to do with me. Because it's an inlander problem. Like someone pulled over for speeding that you pass on a freeway without slowing up or even glancing at. His problem to handle. And this is their problem to handle. And best of luck to them. Because it's a stitch in time sort of thing already come unsewn. But it doesn't really concern me. Birds of a feather sort of a thing. Apples and oranges. There's the sea, and those who live upon her or there is inland, and those who live upon it. But never the twain shall meet. Black and white, oil and water. They want shrimp. I bring them shrimp. They want fish. I bring them fish. They want this. So now I'm bringing them this. But no strings, please. No involvements, please. No associations, please. Because my world stops at the dock, while their world starts at dockside. And cash on delivery. Cash on the barrelhead. No checks. No credit. Because they consume everything they touch without respect. Land. Sea. People. Resources. Users only, them. Not fit company. There goes the neighborhood. So why did you take their mortgage money? Good question, that. And damned near knocked them down in the rush to grab it and run it with the unseen long string. Because of something for nothing. At least you thought it would be. Greed. Green eyed greed. Gimme mine. Gimme, gimme. Because of getting over on inlanders. Any inlander, all inlanders. Anyway, anytime. Oh yes, always that. Turn around. Bend over. Gotcha! At least you thought you could. But then they reeled in that unseen long string. Whoops! and there you were caught, and flopping about gulping. Fish out of water. Prize catch. Spotlighted. Tag, you're it. Musical chairs. Ring around the roses, all fall down. Happy birthday to you, happy birthday to you. Score one for them. One to zip. Yeah, but now you have a special pitch for them aft there in the hold. You're welcome! And many happy returns. Game tied. But they're unstoppable, really. Unbeatable, really, consume, consume, consume. Ooze, flow, devour. Relentlessly. Delaying actions only. Orderly retreats. And they'll legalize this eventually. After the government has milked it sufficiently. After everyone tires of getting in on the act. When the bandwagon grinds to a halt from the overweight. When the preachers and the mob decide so. Which will leave all these narc armies where? High and dry. Holding the bag. Egg on face. Hide and seek ended. Pawns only. April Fool! Game over. Roll over, play dead. Joke on you. Do not pass go, do not collect two hundred dollars. Then a swords to plowshares sort of a thing. And those guys will have to bust ass for a living. Yeah, for a change. Rude awakening, that house of cards. Humpty Dumpty. Leaf in a gale. Here today, gone tomorrow. Tough tit, sucker.

"But meanwhile how will you look docking with lost outriggers and a gashed topsides? Mighty suspicious, like I said. Yeah, mighty suspicious. And how will you explain? Can't. Ain't no way. Because stuttering through a bunch of "well, ahs" just won't do it. No, no help there. Because they definitely ain't idiots. okay, fair warning. Never listen. Mr. Trust. Mr. Assumption. Talk about head buried in sand. But now all of a sudden you don't like any of this. Where have you been? Good morning! Welcome to the real world. Yeah, but roll was called, but you didn't answer.

144

Because you've been here chin deep too late in it. And that's a for sure, for sure. So just keep treading. And just keep hoping that no one makes a wave. And Oscar will fling a proper fit about this damage. And about where you've been, and about what you've been doing. He's like a mother hen when it comes to herself and to yourself. And he'll still be wobbly legging the dock right where you left him. And properly working himself up to that proper fit. But just ignore his sputtering and pouting, his slamming and banging. That'll pass once he sees that you're okay, and that herself can be fixed good as new. Just get him aboard, and fast, then head for Morehead City for repairs, flushing the hold all the way. Herself ain't so well known there. When the repairs are completed we'll haul it for Florida and trawl the Gulf till things here blow over. Or better yet get Oscar, then haul it for Florida. The repairs can be done there. Morehead City is really too close anyway. Yeah, that's better, that's smarter. We'll be in Southport by midafternoon for food and fuel. Then on south, no layovers. Now you're thinking. Wait, Whoa. Whoa. Wait a minute. The bank, you forgot the bank. That's the reason for all this, dummy. Remember? Okay. So mom can make the payment. She'll love doing that. She'll love throwing the megabucks in their inlander faces and saying "there you sons of bitches!" Yeah, but then she'll be a part of this. And you can't have that. She'll be involved if anything goes wrong. No, can't have that. Can't risk that. Okay. All right. Well? What? Okay. So it'll be, go to the dock. By the time me and Oscar get clothes, get food, get fuel, say goodbye to Mom, the bank will be open. I'll go square with them. Then we haul it for Florida. All right. Okay. Yeah, but that will be more time out on a limb. Just that much more time around here looking mighty suspicious. Just that much more time still chin deep and threading. More compromises. More trusting and assuming. And a lot more time hoping for no damn wave. But that's the best way. The only way, really.

"But what about Mary? Well, what about Mary? Nothing about Mary. That's what about Mary. Because we should have had a series of one nighters instead of a marriage. Because Mary's looking for a dick of gold, but all you've got is a lead pipe. Because all commercial fishermen ever have is a wet ass and a hungry gut and a lead pipe dick. And while that's enough for you, it's much too poor too crude for Mary. At least for the long run it is. A sugar and spice and everything nice sort of a thing. A beauty and the beast sort of a thing. A diamonds are a girl's best friend sort of a thing. And while lead pipes are wonderful inventions for rumbles in a bunk, a girl just can't build a future on them. Yeah, but soon you'll have a whole shitpot full of money. So? What difference will that make? None. Not any. Because it'll all go just to clear Bright Dawn's title. Just to stop the damn foreclosure. And Evening Star's title was clear the day she married you. And it was still clear the day she left you. So all you're really doing now is trying to get back to where you started. But minus Mary, of course. But with a far better clear titled trawler. One step back, one step forward. Starting again, but with a big difference. Because with a good catch year Bright Dawn will make four times the money that

Evening Star ever could. Then you can build a rambling house a mile inland where trawlers and the sea are never seen. And the air is always pine scented. And the buffalo roam. And there ain't no discouraging word. And you can shower and put on a suit and tie at the dock before driving there in a long car with tinted windows. And with you plastic wrapped once and for all, Mary will return and consent to being permanently purchased. Because then lead will have become gold. Presto. The wonders of chemistry sort of a thing. But it's really all in the packaging. And you'll have her. And she'll have you. And everything will be just fucking fine. And there we'll go hand in hand down the sunset dusty trail. Happiness, fulfillment, tears, applause, the End. But it ain't only Mary. No one wants commercial fishermen closer than a ten foot pole. Too smelly basic, us. Or raw seafood closer than that either. Too smelly basic, it also. Not convenient enough. Better to sit down to a restaurant's fast food meal of it. No scales. No innards. No gagging cooking odors. Yeah, and spare them the foul sea ordeal of catching it. Just as spare them the stockyards stench and the slaughterers gore behind a steaks fast food restaurant appearance. Packaging, the great sanitizer. And with you prettily wrapped, Mary will be always smiling. And when her inland friends ask where you are, she'll say that you're away on business. And you'll be always smiling also. Because after all it really is only business."

And this was typical of the many wooing conversations over months with Bert Sessions of the Commercial Fisheries Division of the Department of Commerce.

Because when David Midgett came up out of the engine compartment and went down the rollable platform stairs for boats on the railway, then began to long step it across the broken shell and crushed gravel yard of the sprawled marina, Bert Sessions was puppy dog tagging along.

"Then you are David Midgett." Finally having decided.

"The tide wash you up?"

"Huh?"

"No telling what a tide will leave."

"Oh." But already getting winded from not keeping up.

"Look, everyone says you're the best. So you're the captain I must talk with." Beginning to puff and beginning to trail.

"I'm spending money not making money with my boat on the rail."

"Look, can't we sit somewhere and talk?"

But David already was through the front new outboard motor display room of the marina building, through the wide parts department with its rowed cabinets from floor to ceiling of shelves lined with a thousand side by side trays of parts arranged by part number, into the rear mechanics shop area and having already found the special socket size from the shallow drawer of hundreds of them, was coming out while Bert was still coming in then suddenly backward sideways stumbling to get out of David's way and having begun to sweat.

"Look." His way behind voice said. But David was long stepping it across the yard again.

After a while Bert came down the engine compartment ladder and sat on a closed toolbox of various wrenches. But his fresh this morning dress shirt had already died from the sweat.

"Okay if I smoke."

"No oil and fuel spills here. Her bilge is as clean as a supper table."

"You aren't an easy man to talk with."

"Just taking care of business."

"I can understand that."

So David let it lay.

"Look, here's the bottom line." Having gotten his wind again. "We're going to extend the territorial waters to two hundred miles. Then ban all foreign fleets from fishing within it. Atlantic, Pacific, Gulf of Mexico. American Fisheries for American Fishermen."

"Y'all would have been ten years too late with that ten years ago."

"That's history. Now we're going to do it. But our fleet is too few and too small. It simply can't fill the void. We must triple the number of our boats within a year. Boats, right? And triple their size too."

"Now you're talking ships."

"Whichever." Bert being on a roll now.

"The Russian and Japanese Governments can afford ships. But I can't afford a ship."

"The American Government will fix it so you can. At least a hell of a big boat."

"What happens when the wind shifts?"

"I don't understand."

"Things change down here whenever the wind shifts."

"This wind won't shift."

But when the Democratic administration became the Republican administration. When the euphoric commitment of "if we can go to the moon, we can do this" first began to stall then began to fade then just vanished all together. When the planned vast complex of automated seafood processing facilities at the new deepwater port at Wanchese remained largely that, planned, still on the drawing board. When the rapid distribution refrigerated seafood trucking line never really even made it to the planning stage. When the murderously shallow channel at Cape Hatteras was not dredged, nor was it jetted, and trawlers continued to wreck and to break apart on the same deadly shoals. When the spring and the fall migrating fish stocks of all varieties migrated again that year, but in thin gatherings rather than in dense schools for whatever the biological reason. When unloading the recently launched Bright Dawn at the same seafood buyers clogged docks was like a super tanker being unloaded into fifty five gallon drums that then were handcarted to processing. When distribution was still by pickup trucks that had plywood enclosed backs and used air conditioners for refrigeration. When gradually but definitely Bert Sessions became more frequently either "out of the office" or "in conference." When finally none of David' s urgent calls were returned. Then one day a Deputy Sheriff came and served the paper notice that the unforcloseabe mortgage was in fact being foreclosed. So much for guarantees, for promises, for hand shakes. So much for a man's word. And when David appeared before the Clerk of Court but could not show cause why the mortgage should not be foreclosed. Then the foreclosure proceeded on its court ordered impersonal time schedule like an unfolding huge dread that loudly ticks itself off closing in step by closing in step to a doomsday hour end. So much for a solitary man alone with his dream.

Then this was typical of the several enticing conversations during the last weeks with Bobby Willis of the Bogue Inlet Ice and Seafood Company.

"When the hell are you going to repair that damn dock, Bobby!" Coming into the narrow office that was stacked with clutter.

"What's wrong with it'?" From behind his shuffled paperwork desk. But his surprise was not surprise. It was his not caring. And not his not knowing.

"The pilings give a foot. And half the deckplanks are either rotted or missing."

"It's plenty good for awhile yet." Because Bobby Willis was a junky man. And over time everything he ever owned became junky also. Because saltwater is as corrosive to men as it is to material or else as fortifying. Depending on the true character of the man or of the material. Either way saltwater brings it out, sharp and indelible, and fast.

"If Bright Dawn breaks her mooring it's going to be you and me, asshole." Asshole was his other name. But he did not mind that anymore than he minded his junky dock.

"Why should you care, David? They will take her in a couple weeks anyway."

"She's still mine till then,"

"Well, don't hassle me just because the bank has you tied with a hard knot, and you can't get it loose."

"Just get me turned around so I can get the hell away from this piece of shit of a dock."

"I'm short handed. Sometime tomorrow, maybe."

"Today. Get the men."

"Can't afford the cost."

"Well, I can't afford the delay, asshole!"

"Today, tomorrow, day after. What difference does it make, David? You can't stop the foreclosure anyway."

"Not moored to this dock I can't."

"These small catches ain't nothing. You need: the whole nine yards, and you need it now."

"Can't catch more than there is out there to catch."

"Just say the word, and I'll call the man."

"I told you to forget that."

"Then what can I say."

"If you had a suction pump unloading onto a conveyor instead of a man with an ice shovel loading wooden boxes, I could get turned around in an hour."

"Now you're talking a whole other ballgame, David. But the return just ain't there for it."

152

"Well, at least get more men, asshole." The stress showing in harsh forehead lines.

"I said I can't see it."

"Me and Oscar will help."

"Suit yourself. But not more men. The return just ain't there for that either."

"I'll foot the men."

"Oh well, that's different."

"Get them."

"When I've finished these invoices."

"Now!

"What damn difference will it make, David? But the man in Miami is still just a phone call away."

"The men, asshole! Get the men in here!" So Bobby Willis shrugged, then began to get the men. Because what the hell was it to him anyway? Because he already knew as fact what David did not yet even suspect. And if far back David had begun to suspect it like a way off tolling, his conscious still rejected it. But soon David would come to know it as fact, also. Finally, consciously. Because David really could not stop it. Not really. Not with these small catches. Not with these forever taking turn arounds. Maybe with ten quick small catches that combined would total one fairly large catch. Maybe then. Maybe. Maybe with speedy turn arounds. Maybe then. Maybe. But probably not. Not really. Because in foreclosure, time slowly then faster becomes the enemy. The only enemy. Passing time. Ticking time. Clanging time. Footstomp marching time. Clomp. Clomp. Morning. Afternoon. Evening. Night. Morning, afternoon, evening, night. Building speed time. Blurring swiftly time. Thundering by time. Time, time, time. Because a foreclosure is like a train. It, too, must just chug awhile before gaining its steam. Chug, chug, chug. But once it has gained its steam, then look out! Heads up! Stand back! And Katey bar the door! Because now it just puffer steams along like hell fire on steel wheels rolling uphill downhill around curves, makes no matter. Because now it has its full steam ahead. Now it cannot be stopped. Now the Great Wall itself could not stop it. The Great Hordes themselves could not stop it. But heavy money can stop it. Ah yes, that again. Because once again and as always, money talks and bullshit walks. As always, that. Because the government really does not care about the individual. Because the Clerk of Court really does not care about the individual. Because the bank really does not care about the individual. And all because lawyers care only about lawyers. Because lawyers definitely do not care about the individual. So then this was the one blunt conversation that David had with the tough voice that telephoned from Miami.

"You know where thirty four and a half and seventy seven and a quarter is?"

"Yes."

"Thirty five miles out."

"Yes."

"This coming Thursday. Eleven thirty p.m. sharp."

"Okay."

"Repeat, sharp. Exactly there. Exactly then."

"Okay."

"I mean to a gnat's ass."

"All right!"

"Okay. You both approach with no lights. Repeat, no lights."

"Okay."

"You signal first. Running lights only. On two seconds, off three seconds, on two seconds. This repeated three times."

"Okay. "

"Then their signal. Also running lights only. On four seconds, off three seconds, on four seconds. Also repeated three times. okay?"

"Yes."

"Remember it. Do not, repeat, do not write it down."

"Okay."

"It's complicated for good reason."

"Okay."

"Your signal to a gnat's ass, or he'll break and run. His signal to a gnat's ass, or you break and run."

"I've got it."

"Okay. Fulcher's Landing, Queen's Creek. Know where that is?"

"Of course."

"Okay. Trucks, plenty of loaders, arrive there one a.m. Repeat, one a.m. Get there a.s.a.p. Repeat a.s.a.p. Do not play with yourself while coming in. A.S.A.P. Got that?"

"Yes."

"Okay. Quarter mil, small bills, on delivery. Okay?"

"Yes."

"Okay." Then there was a click. And the tough Miami voice was gone. Because a quarter of a million and change is what it would take. This to smash the relentless train dead in it's tracks as though it had crashed a tunnelless mountain head on. Stopped train. Killed train. Smoking rubble. All over. Because a quarter of a million is a heavy talker and a no walker. A pure mountain mover is it. Because David Midgett already had paid in seven hundred and fifty thousand plus most of the interest on principal. This in spite of every odd, every shortcoming, every obstacle, every setback, every failing, every disappointment, this diligently, determinedly, obsessively even, in spite of the aggravation the frustration and toward the last the futility. Commendable yes, bankable no. And at the last it was a simple lapse of integrity, a simply surge of dishonesty, that accomplished what the Hordes themselves, the Wall itself could not have accomplished. A simple resort to crime. Because once that far into foreclosure there then can be no rearrangement, no grace period, no extension, no refinancing, no going back. No nothing. Only a quarter of a million and change payable in full upon demand. or else. However, wherever it is gotten, no questions asked. Only that. No if's, no ands, no buts, no reasons, no excuses, no I think I cans, no rationalizations, no escape. Surely no pity. No, absolutely no pity. Only foreclosure.

Only that relentlessly to deprive the right of a desperate man of redeeming his property. Is foreclosure, is foreclosure, is foreclosure. Ah, but at nine tomorrow morning David Midgett would be at the bank with the smash crash stopper. The Mover. The Killer. The all talker and no walker. Yes hell he would.

But by what shameful means. But by what slinking means. Having that briefly decided, having this quickly done, now comes the long, cold, lonely, living with it. Because it is bad business, this sorry business, this smuggler business. Yes, smuggler business. And smuggler you now are in fact, David, indeed. Though smuggler you can never be in character. Because bluewatermen just do not use the sea so. Because bluewatermen just do not slight the sea so. Because bluewatermen just do not spoil the sea so. Because bluewatermen just do not tarnish the sea so. Because bluewatermen just do not foul the sea so. Therefore bluewatermen never have a reason to cringe upon the sea. Therefore bluewatermen never have a reason to cower upon the sea. Therefore bluewatermen never have a reason to slink upon the sea. As you now slink upon the sea, David. And if there has been a prosperous four hundred year smuggler history along these thousand miles of North Carolina coastline of strung barrier islands, of vast sounds, of wide bays, of winding rivers, of sheltered coves, of hidden creeks, of endless marshes, this has nothing to do with you either. You who were born and raised sailor salty here at the shore where her altar begins. Because bluewatermen are the truest fishermen. Because she is their noble test. Because she is their great challenge. Because she is for the courageous. Because she is for champions. Because she is for heros. So what in the name of all this that is precious, of all this that is sacred, are you doing slinking here upon her, David!

CHAPTER SIX

His hands were stiff now from the wild handling of the bales. They are too weak to even make a fist. The new cuts and the new gouges are sore welts, and matted blood has dried ugly on the deepest of these. His hands are terrible looking hands, even for hard working man's hands. And inside here and out of the worst of the wind and away from the worst of the swells and removed from their demanding immediacy, tender waves of weariness frequently rise within him, and it is only vigorous head shakes that prevent him from being gently drawn further within by them to drift to dream to sleep. What a harsh night, what a frantic night, what an exhausting night. But more night remains. But still he wants it ended. This night of all the nights, ended. Because his body is beyond weary. Because his mind is beyond weary. But more night remains. But still he wants it ended this night of all the nights, ended. But more night remains. To end soon, but not yet. But the sliver moon already is setting. It has not been much of a moon this night anyway. But the stars still are bright. They have had a wonderful night. They have enjoyed themselves, those stars have. So he is piloting herself by their light only. The inland waterway is like a long canal. And a canal is like a long road. With a long road and no opposing traffic, all you do is keep it between the banks. So he is simply keeping herself between the banks. Besides starlight reflects well off water, so the water is lighter. But starlight does not reflect well off the stunted trees and twisted scrubs that are on both banks, so the banks are darker. But still it is a matter of shades rather than a matter of clarity. Because when your eyes have learned to distinguish shades and you practice these distinctions then no light boat night piloting becomes quite natural, because being accurately aware of shaded objects is the same thing as actually seeing the objects clearly. Because he can even distinguish the dark house shapes and sizes and their recesses and their protrusions and their different levels there among the taller trees and the grass yards that have begun well back on the higher ground of the inland bank now that Queens Creek is not very much further ahead. But he probably should on herself's running lights anyway to avoid attracting the suspicion of any chance late night cannot sleeper and out walking arounder. He will in a minute. And he is keeping herself just beyond the powerful searchlight limit of the deep rumble working tug that is bulldozer pushing a low in the water loaded fuel barge there several hundred yard astern. But any trouble that may come would come from ahead. But still he feels more secure from surprise, at least from that direction, with the tug and the barge there where they are taking up almost the entire channel and in effect are thereby blocking it. And besides, a well skiff had been running the waterway, hugging the inland bank for the past mile or more and he has been keeping it about one hundred yards ahead as a sort of happen chance and unsuspecting pointman. And when the fisherman in the well skiff turned on his pipe stand worklight amidship to stow loose and can get in the way gear, David could see the carefully hauled in and neatly folded gillnet that lay still seawater sparkling across the transom. Ah, so the fisherman has been sink netting a known to him fish run at the mouth of a small bay during the just passed high water slack. Yes, that is what has him out and about and so busy during the dead of this night. And during the slack because then there will not be a fast moving tide for the net to snake in and tangle foul itself. And equally as important during the slack because the fish that have come inshore from the sea tend to go into small bays on high tide to feed then to go out to deeper channel water on low tide for safety. So the fish move past a specific location during the slacks. But the fish have favorite small bays and they change favorite small bays according to their instinctive whim, so it is the fisherman's secret and the fisherman's skill to know which favorite small bay the fish are in. But there is a hell of a lot of luck to it also, and no secret and no skill and simply being at the right small bay at the right time. So David wished the fisherman luck. All the best luck that one commercial fisherman would wish another commercial fisherman. But a professional courtesy wish is all that it could be, because the well skiff is riding too high in the water and it is running too fast. So no swamping fish load and no luck and so far a mighty lean night's work for the fisherman. But then with the stiff steady onshore wind this had been a flood high tide rather than a normal high tide and therefore a whole lot of fish moving around room in the flood water at the specific location. But home and warm and dry and a nap and breakfast then the fisherman will be back out with his net sunk for the low water slack that will be at dawn. Because a skiff about to swamp from the fish load is always going to happen with the next tide slack. Always. And now and then it really does happen. So David said "hang in there, fella." But the fisherman would anyway because that is what commercial fisherman do.

It is at this moment that the fisherman stands with a hand held spotlight to search ahead to be absolutely certain that he is not running too close bankside to the stubby private boatdocks that have begun now that the houses have begun. But lighted there at the very limit of the spotlight is a Coast Guard twin outboard runabout with its diagonal international orange for quick recognition wide strip marking from its bow aft tied to a stubby dock just before the mouth of Queens Creek. The three Guardsmen in international orange also all weather jumpsuits with black bolstered forty fives black belted around their waists casually standing about the runabout's workdeck waiting. The posed ready runabout loosely tied bow out and waiting also. Waiting! There ahead waiting! "Oh shit!" said David as immediately he cuts herself 's power to idle. Because ass puckering fear time is suddenly here with a rush. Because think don't panic, think don't panic time is suddenly here for sure, for sure. "It's a trap" said David. And it is. "I've been given over" said David. And he had. Then the spotlight is offed. Only the dark night is ahead. But that does not change a damn thing. Because things simply do not disappear just because of dark. Because the Guardsmen and whoever the hell else are still there ahead at the mouth of Queens Creek. They were not offed when the spotlight was offed. They are still there. Waiting. Yes they are. Yes hell they are! And for him. For our himself hisself. "Well you may as well put your head between your legs and kiss your ass goodbye" said David. "Because you're caught now." And he is. "Well, do something! Anything!" said David. "But something!" Because our two are about to be silhouetted by the fast approaching now tug's searchlight. But the Guardsmen had looked so they are temporarily blinded by the spotlight. And too our two are expected to come from the opposite direction. Because these particular Guardsmen are the back door of the trap and not the front door of the trap. But the barge will have run down our two before David could get himself turned about. And herself is simply too conspicuous simply too obvious like waving a flag, hey here we are, to even attempt to run the waiting trap while ridiculously trying to play the innocent. So with no other alternative at this moment and having to immediately do something, anything, but something anyway, David gives herself power and spins the wheel and makes a starboard turn through a dense scrubline of short trees and into the channel that runs through Spooners Bay.

But Spooners Bay in only a wide place like a flat fish bulge in a heron's stretched neck, that is midway into this mile long channel that runs straight and narrow from the waterway to behind Bear Island. And a wide place that is shallow on both sides of the channel, with bottoms that are thick sea grassy in their halved middles, that themselves are boarded with barren packed sand and embedded dead shells along their banks, and together these halfs have been always abundant for scalloping and for clamming and for gillnetting and for shrimping for the bay skiff fishermen. And in the old times the Spooner family owned it by virtue of a land grant, before the State took possession of this as well as all coastal wetlands and estuaries for the public good and for the public's use, that lie brown green sprawled vast and marine nursery life rich between the mainland and the barrier islands. Bear Island is a barrier island, but it has long been State owned because of a farsighted early will, and it is a three mile long sea oat wavy and wind gnarled tree wilderness world of its very own with Bogue Inlet at one end and Bear Inlet at the other end, and in the still earlier old times it actually had been a favorite bear home that is and until bears got into a pissing contest with the first white man that never really was much of a contest to begin with. But the channel through Spooners Bay does not have a name until it tees with Cow Channel, that is narrow also but much less straight, that runs the length behind Bear Island where the flat wetlands stop and the becoming high dunes begin. And in the more recent old times, but before the farsighted will and before the waterways dredging, Bear Island was the drop point for mail ordered cattle that were delivered by the Norfolk to Charlestown and towns in between bulk freight boats. Because these boats had too much draft for the inlet and the bay waters at Swansboro, so they would run in close to the surf off Bear Island beach, then simply shove off the wagon grease smeared against winter damp and cold or summer flies and mosquitoes cattle that then made the beach rather wild eyed and loud hollering, and only a little worse for the wear to graze about the island until the receiving farmer with friends came to herd them into Cow Channel, thus its name, and to low tide swim them to their mainland new home. But while these teeing channels are just fine for cattle swimming and they are just fine for here about skiff working and they are just fine for quick access to the white sandy bottoms inside Bogue and Bear Inlets for the Queens Creek flounder giggers, they certainly are not just fine for big trawler maneuvering like an ocean liner seeking to navigate teeing canals because this would be like trying to move a three pound vessel through a two pound ditch.

But this is exactly the situation in which David finds himself. Because when you absolutely must get off a cannot go forward, cannot go backward congested and still closing street, your natural reaction is to dart suddenly into an alley, any alley. But now here in the alley David cannot back out then return the way he came, the return to New River Inlet way, even though the tug dozer pushing the barge has already gone by, even though this choice is the most logical is the wisest, is by far the best choice, because this alley channel is simply too narrow for nighttime, anytime for that matter, backing by a big trawler such as our's certainly, assuredly even, because at some point herself's stern would be accidently unavoidably ram stuck into the close on either side mudbank bending the props and the shafts and stranding our two and thus ending this cat and mouse gotcha game prematurely. So we have a true caught between a rock and a hard place sort of a thing. For sure. But David must do something. David has to do something. Anything. But something. And now, right now. But what? 'I just don't know,' thinks David. Anything damn it! "Jesus, here we go again," says David. But something. Because this voyage will not end, and he wants it to end. Because this night will not end, and he wants it to end. Because he only wants to get rid of this fifteen tons of marijuana, but he cannot get rid of this fifteen tons of marijuana. Because he only wants the quarter of a million, but he cannot get the quarter of a million. Because he wants to again be safe, to again be secure, to again be on firm land. Because he is sore and cold and weary and hungry and confused and scared and lonely and sick now of this whole sorry bad wrong damn business. Because he is trapped, and he is caught. Because there is no way out, and he knows that there is no way out. But he has to find a way out, he must find a way out, because there is a way out, there has to be a way out, there must be a way out. And it can be found and it must be tried at least tried, because it is not impossible because it is possible. So he says "think damn it, think!" because he must plan, he must consider, then he must decide, then he must do simply go ahead and do it and without thinking about it then. Because he cannot be scared and cold and sick and weary and confused and sore and hungry and lonely any longer. At least not now. Later he can be all these. And other things even. But not now. Not now and not one of these not any of these not none of these. And there no longer is a brother Harold, judgmental toward him there far inland beside the Tar River. And there no longer is a wife Mary and young son, estranged from him there far inland also. Because with this criminal act and its repercussions those chapters are ceased. And there no longer is a mate Oscar loyal to him close by on the dock at the marina, and there no longer is a mother, Mom high tider splendid for him close by also at Swansboro though these chapters will resume in spite of this criminal act and its repercussions.

So for now and for this while there in only himself here atop herself and our two completely isolated and left to their own cunning, left to their own devices, this while mule hauling the three point nine million in suddenly worthless cargo that now must be sea dumped. What other choice is there? Because it is not deliverable as addressed. Because there is no forwarding address. Because it cannot be returned to sender. Because it cannot be package binned to await a change of address. Because it together with our two were given over while enroute. So for the present they are merely awaited for and in ambush. But soon they will be actively sought. Soon they will be fugitives. Soon they will be hunted. And by all available means. By helicopters. even. And once hunted along this coast there quickly becomes so very few places to hide. Really hide. Because what had been vast has become small. Especially because of helicopters. So this one minute priceless cargo, has become worthless cargo in the next minute, and it must be sea dumped like so much trash, like so much garbage. what other choice is there? Then the hold thoroughly seawater flushed.

Then finally sore body home and at last weary to bed. And to hell with explanations because he cannot be charged with evidence that cannot be found. Then somehow resolve the foreclosure another day and in another way. Then the rigging repairs so to trawl again. But first there is the getting back to sea. Ah yeah, that. Formidable that. Huge that. Looming that. But not impossible that. No, not impossible. At least it must be tried. At least tried. Because again and above all and forever true, bluewatermen do persevere. Yes, always that.

Because with this all night blowing a pure gale onshore wind, there is still this high tide that is a flood tide. Because when a door is closed, a window is opened. Sometimes. Usually even. Maybe this time. Possibly this time. Hopefully this time. Because there are seven hundred and seven low tides a year just as there are seven hundred and seven high tides a year, but with no two tides exactly alike whether here or at any other tidal area throughout the world. Because with variations for wind direction and velocity as well as earth rotation as well as moon gravitation, the tidal extremes remain approximately six hours apart and within these periods the rule of twelfths applies, so that beginning with a high tide slack, one twelfth passes out during the first hour, and two twelfths during the second four, and three twelfths during each of the third and fourth hours, then two twelfths again, then one twelfth again, then low water slack. It is during the middle two hours that the water passes at its swiftest, and this comprises half of the fall. And our high water slack was an hour ago. So the water has really only just begun to pass. So maybe this is an opened window, now that the door has been closed. Maybe. Possibly. Hopefully. Because high tide was a two foot higher flood tide than a normal high tide. But herself draws eight feet of water when as fully loaded as this. And there is no way in hell that there is eight feet of water, even with this flood tide, all the way along this channel through Spooners Bay, to the tee behind Bear Island, then out through Cow Channel to the inlet. No, no way in hell. But the two twelfths hour has only just begun with the two three twelfths hours still to come. Three good hours. The three best hours. If, yes, if. And there can be good in narrow, together with the bad that is in narrow. Because narrowed so, confined so, channeled so, the water will pass out of here like stampeded mustangs headed for the draw as it drives, gathers, pushes, sweeps, carries, all the everything with it before it in twisting swirls in rolling eddies. Because the volume that is to pass will damn well pass, and right now nothing and no one and not anything can stop it, can divert it, can slow it even. So if David can get herself beyond the inlet before the end of the third hour, then gaining the free sea again just may be possible. Escaped and loosed and no longer trapped.

But the list of if's has begun to fill a page. Because along the tee half of Cow Channel that runs to Bogue Inlet, there is a sharp bend that is a literal corner, and herself's length is too long to make that corner. Cannot cram this three pound vessel through that two pound place. No way. Slam, another door is closed. So if there really is an opened window, then it would have to be along the other half of Cow Channel, that runs to Bear Inlet. But Bear Inlet has never been anything except an inlet in name only, on charts only, for small boats only, because all of the shallow channels that run from inside, bay side, half circle to it are too narrow just as this shallow channel is too narrow. Trawlers have never tried it, because why would they need to try it with wide deep Bogue Inlet so sea accessible there, not until now, not until this trawler our trawler.   But is the bar at Bear Inlet too shoaled for passage?   Who knows. No one has ever needed to know. No one has ever cared enough to find out. At least there are only easy bends along this half of Cow Channel to it. At least that. But can he pass through them in time, with time now increasingly becoming the real enemy? Who knows. There will be eight feet of water and more in the frequent holes, in the frequent current cuts along the way. But certainly not at the upside of both banks. No, certainly not there. But if, just if David proceeds herself ahead very slowly, very carefully, delicate feelingly even, then when herself does begin to mudbank side or sandbar middle run aground then he can gently duck waddle her wheel from side to side, so that herself gently duck waddles from side to side also, and continues to maintain forward progress by feet, by inches even, and is never allowed to stick stuck finally, then maybe just maybe herself can gouge her own channel through the shallows. Because with the swift driving sweeping push that it has, the stampeded water will churn and dig and move away the thick silt the clutching sand from before her, from beneath her, from around her. But imagine the skill that this will require, and imagine the experience that this will require, and imagine the daring that this will require, and image the patience that this will require. But then desperate men attain where secure men fail. And faint heart never wins fair maiden. Or is it really a fools rush in sort of a thing? Who knows. But it must be tried. Yes, at least tried. What other choice is there? So David said yet another outloud "Jesus, here we go again."

But the window that we hoped had been opened, when the doors were closed, turned out to be only a broad vista window, a picture window, a go to and see out of window, and not a climb through and get out of window. Because herself is hard aground on the bar at Bear Inlet. And all around, the water had the pale blue clearness that it has in close sandy bottoms. And ahead there is the surf that is white foamy as it continually beats itself upon the outside of the bar. No, no inlet this. Probably never had been. Probably never will be. Another door this, the final door this. And beyond there, is the calm now windy darkness of the deep sea. So himself said "I'm sorry, lady", and he gave her big wheel a last caress. Because the escape is ended, because the try is ended, because the voyage is ended. So himself goes aft to the galley and from the refrigerator gets a six pack of beer and pulls one free from its plastic holder and tab opens it and drinks it. Then from a foil wrapped package from the refrigerator also he gets a tall one hand stack of fried cold now pork chops and begins slowly to eat them. No hurry now, all the time in the world now. Dawn is still an hour away. So relax, enjoy, ponder. Only these now. All these now.

Because they do not know where the hell he is. Only that he is long overdue. Only that he is somewhere. But where? They are there scratching their balls with one hand and picking buggers from their noses with the other hand, and wondering where the hell he is. That is funny. That's riot. Because he knows where is he is. And soon he will let them know also. At least where he had been. Because the helicopters will be out and about at dawn. So he has until then. Plenty of time. All the time in the world time. Time to eat, time to drink, time to collect personals, time to get herself ready. Plenty of time. A lifetime of time.

Because there is only the new dawn walk for him to make the length of Bear Island, here beside his sea and her thrill and in her winds that have slackened that have stilled. And this will be a walk toward something, rather than a walk away from something. Because Red Mauldin will be bringing the Billy Anna through Bogue Inlet in the early morning after a three day trawl between here and Topsail island. And he will hail Red from the inlet beach and Red will slow, and he will swim out and Red will be surprised and he will explain. Then he will stay out of sight aboard at the dock and sleep his weary sleep while Red goes and tells Oscar and Mom. Then Oscar will come and be out of sight aboard also. And in the evening, Mom will come with packed suitcases for the trip, and to say her goodbyes for the long while that it will be. Then in the morning when Red has the Billy Anna turned around for a trawl off South Carolina, he and Oscar will go south with Red, because he would do it for Red, so Red will do it for him, because Red also has only the sea. And when Red is sufficiently south, he and Oscar will be at night offshore transferred to another trawler that is working her way even further south to off Georgia and Florida, until finally he and Oscar will be through the Caribbean and down along the bulge of the South American coast. And once there, a stranger businessman will gladly loan him a rusty old wooden trawler for him and Oscar to work on shares, because whether he can regularly fully load a trawler with fresh seafood is the only important question, and is all that is wanted to know. Meanwhile they will definitely know where our herself is. Yes, that immediately and that spectacularly. But they will not know where the hell he is. That is funny. That Is a riot. But that is the way that it should be. Because it is their laws, and they can have them. They and the horde of all the other theys also. And it is their banks and they can have them, and it is their government and they can have that, and it is their congestion and they can have that, and it is their pollution and they can have that, and it is their invasion and they can have that. Since they desire all these, so shall they have all these. His present to them, and lots of luck. Because none of it ever really had anything to do with him. No, not really.

So ready now with dawn beginning now, with his personals and with Oscar's personals, and with the three beers remaining from the six pack, collected and in a canvas tote bag beside the bow hatch, he went below to the engine compartment. And with a pipe wrench he loosed the twin fuel lines from the tanks, so that the remaining one thousand gallons of diesel fuel could drain into the

173

bilge opening. Below again, with a bunk blanket and with a can of cook stove alcohol, the tanks had emptied. So he dropped the blanket on the deck and poured the alcohol over it, then kicked the blanket into the opening. Then he dropped in a lighted match and there was the strong whoosh of the alcohol soaked blanket's ignition, so he went topside opening vents and sliding open ports as he went, for the good draft that these would produce.

Forward now, he overboarded the bowline then went and slid the bow hatch cover to complete the good draft and arm slung the tote bag. Then he overboarded himself and hand holded his way down the bowline, and into the before waist deep water now knee deep water.

What a great fire this will be. A magnificent fire, a spectacular fire, a monumental fire even. And monuments should attract attention. And this monument certainly would attract attention. The alcohol soaked blanket giving the thousand gallons of diesel fuel the agent assisted ignition start that it needs. The diesel fuel giving the fifteen tons of structural fiberglass the agent assisted ignition start that it needs. And together the fuel and the fiberglass giving the three hundred bales of seawater soaked marijuana the agent assisted ignition start that it needs. An all day burn for sure, for sure. The tall flames visible for ten miles. The dense smoke visible for fifty miles. And burning so roaringly hot and in so awkwardly remote a place that there will be no choice but to let it burn. Burn lady burn. Literally inferno hot until even the engines themselves melt. The rolling skyward billowing black toxic smoke of the petroleum.   The rolling skyward billowing white narcotic smoke of the marijuana. What a downwind high. What a downwind kick in the head. Another present from him to them and best of luck.   And when the fuel is consumed and when the marijuana is consumed and when the resin is consumed from the fiberglass only herself's hull will remain there below the waterline in the clear sandy bottom as a bold monument to futile perseverance. Then obscure Bear Inlet will have become forever famous as the grave of Bright Dawn, the wonder trawler, and from where David Midgett, the outlaw captain, simply vanished.   From ashes to ashes. From the sea to the sea. So he stood on the inlet beach and watched herself afire just as any bystander would watch any fire. In a while he turned and walked away no longer even curious. After all, what was it to him. Because he had tried. Yeah, the stupid son of a bitch had tried.

www.ingramcontent.com/pod-product-compliance
Lightning Source LLC
Chambersburg PA
CBHW030508260626
47157CB00005B/1707